IN THE BLOOD

A Peter Sinclair Prequel

John Wingate

Also in the Submariner Sinclair Series

Submariner Sinclair

Jimmy-The-One

Sinclair in Command

Nuclear Captain

Sub-zero

Full Fathom Five

IN THE BLOOD

Published by Sapere Books.

20 Windermere Drive, Leeds, England, LS17 7UZ,
United Kingdom

saperebooks.com

ISBN: 978-1-80055-301-9

They that go down to the sea in ships: and occupy their business in great waters;
These men see the works of the Lord: and His wonders in the deep.

TO
OUR SEAFARERS
UPON WHOM THIS NATION DEPENDS FOR ITS LIFEBLOOD.

ACKNOWLEDGEMENTS

The author wishes to acknowledge with gratitude the kindness of the British Shipping Federation under whose auspices all doors were opened to him. His thanks are also due to the Officers at the Westcliff-on-Sea Merchant Service School; the Captain Superintendent and Staff of The Gravesend Sea School; and to all those others who went out of their way to make the task easier for him.

Particularly, the author wishes to thank the Port Line Shipping Company and Shell Tankers Ltd., for their generous and unstinted help. Lastly, he wishes to record his gratitude to those at sea who extended overwhelming hospitality and true friendship. Without their forbearance and encouragement, this story would never have been written.

CHAPTER 1: A HOUSE DIVIDED

A drizzle was falling as Peter Sinclair, one of the year's new apprentices, pushed his cycle through the gates of Giles and Brown, Makers of Precision Tools. The darkness of a winter dawn accentuated the garish pools of light from the neon tubes which overhung the Security Department's office: Peter watched the diagonal traceries of water slashing past the lights which threw into profile the queue sluggishly recording its existence by the ritual of clocking-in. Bang! Thump! A glance at the indelible record on the card and Sinclair P., Apprentice, had begun another day's grind at Giles and Brown.

''urry up, lad. We ain't got all day.' The bronchial voice of an elderly fitter wheezed behind him, a man disliked by the apprentices: he was a bully and relished pushing the youngsters around, a pleasure in which he could indulge easily because he was the machine shop foreman under whom most of them spent their training.

'What's the hurry?' a younger voice growled from the rear of the queue. 'We've got the whole rotten day, haven't we, Mr Hodge?' The youth was large, with heavy shoulders and a matt of flaxen hair. The tone of his reply was sarcastic and infuriating. The young man's contempt was not lost on Mr Hodge who spat into the gutter. The foreman pushed his hands deeper into the pockets of his donkey jacket and, slinging his dinner bag further on to his shoulder, strode out of the light and into the darkness towards the silhouettes of the workshops.

'I'll be seein' you later, MISTER Finnimore,' he growled and he spat again, this time aiming towards the young man's feet.

Peter Sinclair stacked his cycle in the rack and, hurrying to catch up Finnimore, overtook him as they entered the sliding doors of the machine shop. The vast area was brightly illuminated and the two young men blinked as they took stock of what were now becoming familiar surroundings.

Peter Sinclair, nearly seventeen, appeared taller than he was, a bare six foot. This illusion was partly because he stood slightly poised on the balls of his feet, like a natural boxer. His shoulders were square rather than broad and the frame of his body tapered to the narrow hips of the athlete. He was dark, the fashion of the time dictating a mop of black hair surrounding his square-cut face, though he did limit his sideboards to sensible proportions; at least the hair was a luxuriant growth, unlike Morgan Finnimore's fungus which wispily encompassed the sides of his cheeks.

Peter's brown eyes were set wide apart beneath bushy, black eyebrows. His steady gaze implied a directness that emphasized the lips which, though full and generous, were moulded into a firm line. His face was purposeful, some might call it stubborn, though he would have preferred to feel that he was ambitious and determined to make a success of his life. He stood back to allow Finnimore to pass between him and the door as they strolled towards the hooks on the wall where the apprentices hung their belongings.

'Sorry, Pete, but this one's the only hook left; stick yours on Old Podge's.'

Morgan Finnimore had bestowed the foreman with this nickname and had seen to it that Hodge discovered the fact from the junior apprentice, Ned Hindacre, apparently a feeble individual, too sensitive by far to stand up to Hodge's bullying.

Finnimore, Peter had soon realized, was too slick to be trusted but they had both joined Giles and Brown at the same time and so had inevitably been thrown together. Morgan Finnimore had assumed a cavalier attitude towards Peter, a take-it-or-leave-it offer of friendship. Being of easy-going temperament, Peter had accepted the relationship, for Finnimore was undoubtedly the 'goer' amongst the apprentices: he knew all the wrinkles, was first to stand up to Hodge, learned how to dodge the authorities when they came snooping to check on the work-rate; but, thought Peter, slyness was already beginning to show in Morgan Finnimore's face.

The flaxen hair was streaky and would have benefited from a wash. The forehead beneath the untidy mop was obscured but Finnimore was undoubtedly clever, if animal cunning could be termed intelligence. The closeness of the pale blue eyes rarely betrayed emotion. Peter would have hated to make an enemy of his erstwhile companion. Allied to Morgan's natural intelligence was his brute strength: a massive, lion-like head protruded from a thick neck that jutted from shoulders humped above his barrel of a chest. The torso was thick and, in spite of the six-foot-three of his height, his legs seemed like tree trunks.

'Watch out. Here comes Podge.' Finnimore was gazing soulfully upwards at the lights; he stuck his hands in his pockets as the foreman strode aggressively towards them.

'C'mon, my lad; you'll be late.' He made as if to hang his World War II gas-mask haversack on the hook marked 'Foreman', but the space was already occupied by a bag marked, 'P. Sinclair'. He turned, flushing with anger, and glowered at Peter.

'Move that bleedin' bag.'

Peter jerked towards the hook and was about to remove the offending article when Finnimore spoke, without raising his voice: 'Leave it where it is, Peter. The hook belongs to the company: it's not Mr Hodge's private property.'

Peter was about to acquiesce when he glimpsed a gleam of amusement in Finnimore's eyes. Peter realized his danger even as Morgan winked. He removed his gear.

'Who the 'ell d'you think you are?' Hodge snarled at Peter before rounding on Morgan. 'Get to your lathes before I report you to the shop steward.'

Finnimore, hands in pockets, sauntered off towards his lathe on the far side of the shop, whistling as he went. Peter followed, ashamed at the puerility of the incident and upset for allowing himself to be influenced so easily by Finnimore. He was silent as he checked his machine, his sensibility acutely aware of his surroundings as he began his sixty-fourth day at Giles and Brown. The smell of the sperm oil percolating from the tempering shop; the hiss of the fast-running machines; the acrid fumes from the spirals of waste metal as the cutting tools bit into the job — all these would be reminders of his apprenticeship all his life, of the discipline of the clock, of the harshness of discontented men, chained monotonously to their life's routine of watching revolving wheels, eternally turning…

Peter Sinclair had to admit that he was frustrated and, like Morgan Finnimore at the adjoining lathe, bored beyond measure. Allowed no initiative whatever, clocking in, clocking out; day in, day out, always the same, their little lives revolving like the lathe wheels, remorselessly, until the Final Depreciation wrote off their lives, when the Chief Accountant finally rendered the balance sheet.

Peter cursed as he saw his cutting tool bite too far into the metal. As he stopped the lathe, he knew that his mistake had not passed unnoticed: he looked round and there he was, Hodge himself, a sneer on his face.

'Daydreaming again, eh, Sinclair?' He elbowed Pete away from the lathe and, producing a steel rule from his breast pocket, measured the length of the job; then, satisfied, he held out his hand towards the apprentice.

'Callipers?'

Peter fumbled in his pocket and wished that he was dead. He'd forgotten even to open the callipers, so distant had been his thoughts.

'So you reckon you can machine by eye, do you?' the foreman grunted. 'No wonder you're flippin' useless. You're worse than Ned Hindacre — and he's in big trouble.'

Peter remained silent and waited for Hodge to move on. He studied the pockmarked face of the foreman. Would he, Peter, have those bitter, turned-down creases at the corner of his mouth when he was in his fifties?

The whistle went. It was breaktime already — those ten minutes when men congregated for a quick 'cuppa'. Already a group of apprentices was forming like bees around a hive and buzzing with eager chatter. In the centre was Ned Hindacre, pale and embarrassed by the sudden attention. From the babble Morgan Finnimore's voice rang out sharply.

'Shut up everyone. Let Ned have his say.'

A few ribald asides petered out and then Hindacre, nervously gaining confidence as he watched the others hanging on his words, recounted the drama of the morning.

Last night he had passed through the gate and, by disastrous mischance, the security officer had asked to see the contents of his bicycle bag. He had always been a model railway enthusiast (and the pale face smiled sheepishly) and spent every spare second at home constructing model steam locos. Yesterday, at the lathe, having an excess of machine oil remaining at the end of the day, he had filled up a small medicine bottle, which he had expressly brought with him, with the fine lubricating oil that he would have thrown into the gash bucket.

Retribution had been swift: he was to forfeit three months of his indentures or he could choose to leave. As soon as the shop stewards had wind of the decision, a meeting was held and, after dinner today, the whole factory would down tools — 'all out' in defiance of management and in support of the apprentice.

Peter watched Ned's face, now an ashen grey.

'I did it, I know,' he said quietly, 'and I deserve what's coming.' He shrugged his shoulders in despair. 'Finnimore's trying to force me to say that someone else planted the oil bottle — but no one did.'

Ned's eyes were filling with tears and he turned away to munch his sandwiches in a solitary corner. Peter wandered towards him and said:

'Cheer up, Ned. We're all behind you.'

A voice broke in, jarring in its harshness.

'Oh, no we aren't.' It was Finnimore who, unnoticed, had been listening on the outside of the circle. 'If the little perisher's going to scab on us, we'll send him to Coventry.'

Day succeeded miserable day: Peter sided with Ned Hindacre but his support soon landed Peter also in the Coventry corner. Arriving at seven o'clock one morning, the two youths were banished for the remainder of the day from all conversation and contact with the rest of the workforce. For Peter, this ostracism bred a slow anger and contempt for the factory society in which he worked; but for Ned Hindacre, the effect was corrosive and, to Peter's eyes, tragic.

'They told me last night they're striking tomorrow if the bosses don't sack me.' Ned spoke with his head averted so that, even if the walls had ears, no one but Peter could have overheard him. Peter grunted, where they stood remotely in a corner, chewing sandwiches during the morning break,

'They can't sack you,' Peter murmured. 'Management won't allow it.'

Hindacre looked long at his friend.

'D'you really believe that?'

Peter reluctantly shook his head.

'Management's lost complete control in this factory; the commies do what they like, leading the rest of us along like a flock of sheep, "Closed shop" is their war cry.'

'Peter…'

Ned paused, then shyly touched Peter's arm. 'If they sack me, I'm finished.' He paused, searching Peter's face. 'What'll my Dad say?'

'He'll understand; he's worked in this set-up.'

'He won't forgive me — it was hard enough getting an apprenticeship here.'

There was a note of desperation in Ned's voice and Peter suddenly felt frightened at what his newly-found friend might do.

'There're other factories, Ned, with stronger management,' Peter said.

'I'd rather be sacked,' Ned concluded lamely. 'At least I'll have stood up to those…' and, for the first time in his life, Ned Hindacre swore with gusto.

'You talking to me, eh, blackleg?' Hodge had a habit of sneaking up unobserved, but this time there was an air of triumph about him. 'The manager wants to see you, Hindacre. C'mon, lad, straight to his office.'

They fired the young Ned Hindacre without further ado. Peter Sinclair, not for the first time in his life, acted on impulse. To the accompaniment of jeers and catcalls, he walked the length of the shop floor to the manager's office.

'You can sack me too,' he said. 'I want no part of this set-up.'

When he had quit the factory gates he felt strangely clean. He'd stood up to the test and had not been found wanting. Suddenly, he was a man.

A grey-haired man in his fifties, Peter's father had survived six years at sea during World War II. When finally he came ashore, he had yearned for the comradeship of a ship's company and had found difficulty in settling down in his civilian job. It was not difficult for him to understand his son's dilemma, when Peter had returned disconsolate from Giles and Brown.

The elder man, leaning forward from his chair, had listened patiently, while waiting for his son to finish recounting the day's events.

'I'm fed up with the constant moaning. If that's all there is to life, there's not much to it. What can I do, Dad?'

Peter, who was by the fire and slumped in the other chair, watched the elder man puffing at his pipe.

'It isn't really their fault, Pete…' his father said. 'It's bad leadership that's just as much to blame — it's the same at sea.'

There was a pause and then, deliberately, the father turned his chair towards the window. He rose, poked at the log fire which, spluttering and spitting, suddenly blazed into life to throw dancing reflections across the windowpanes which, now that Sinclair Senior had drawn back the curtain and turned out the light, were mirroring the leaping flames.

'I'm going to tell you a thing or two about life at sea — if you want to listen, that is, Pete?'

Peter nodded. His father then talked of his naval life, when the sea was always master whether the nations were at peace or at war. He told of the courage of the men of the merchant service who, their ships the primary targets of the U-boats, continued to man their dwindling fleets.

'They were very ordinary men, but they beat Hitler,' Peter's father said. 'The seafaring man is a different animal. I suppose it's a love of one's ship that does it. You all sink or swim together.'

He paused and knocked out his pipe. The younger man turned towards him and together they shared the long silence. The firelight flickered about the room as the grey-haired man concluded:

'That's the brotherhood of the sea, my son. Ordinary blokes, serving a common purpose; but the comradeship is strong enough for them to die for each other.'

He rose from his chair and quietly left the room. Peter sat for a long while before the dying fire. As he stared at the glowing embers, a sense of relief slowly enveloped him. He knew then what he wanted to do with his life.

CHAPTER 2: CALL OF THE SEA

Peter Sinclair stood for a moment on the steps outside Lime Street Station, his gaze absorbing the sharp outline of the buildings in the centre of the city of Liverpool. A girl smiled at him as she glanced up from the pavement below and he grinned sheepishly to himself. For a moment he had forgotten that he was now a different individual from that of a few weeks ago: then he had belonged to that brotherhood of aimless youth which, by its slovenly appearance, reflected more accurately than Peter cared to admit, its total lack of self-respect. Now, after only a fortnight's induction course at the Kingston-upon-Hull Nautical College, he was secretly enjoying this newly-found pride in himself and the standards represented by the uniform he was wearing. He sneaked a glance at his reflection in the plate-glass window display at the side of the station entrance.

The serge of his reefer jacket and smartly creased trousers made him look taller than he was as he stood hesitantly on the steps, a naval blue raincoat over one arm, his travelling grip suspended from his other hand. His cap bore a white cover and the badge of the Haven Shipping Company: gilt laurel leaves enclosing the Company's flag which was a blue St Andrew's Cross on a red ground. He now had a reasonable haircut and, for the first time in his life, he experienced that feeling of pride which identification with something worthwhile can bring to a person. He squared his shoulders and, nipping down the steps, threaded his way through the stream of traffic snaking around the centre of the city.

'It's a different way of life, Peter,' his father had said on that decisive evening, 'and one that demands the most of a man.' Already, during those fourteen hectic days in the Nautical School at Hull, he had begun to understand his father's remark. The instructors who had conducted the induction course were a different breed of men from those who had been running Giles and Brown. They were time-expired seafarers, men who had finally 'swallowed the anchor' to take up a life ashore. The discipline they implanted on their youthful charges was not as harsh as Peter had expected, but the motley collection of youth which had originally assembled was swiftly transformed into a tightly-knit group of keen cadets eager to go to sea.

The enthusiasm was infectious: no longer griping as he did at the factory about every facet of the daily round, Peter absorbed the picture presented to them of life in the Merchant Navy. The shipping industry and life in a ship had been described: all sorts and conditions of ships and the fleets in which they belonged. Peter had learnt to think of a ship as female, and he no longer was going to live 'on' a boat, but 'in' a ship. 'Stairs' became 'ladders', and 'floors' became 'decks'; the cadets were beginning to feel contemptuous of their cousins, the landlubbers.

Now Peter's footsteps led him inevitably, as all the streets in Liverpool seemed to do, towards the Liver Building, that tall pinnacle of dark, forbidding masonry on top of which perched the Liver Bird, traditionally the seafarer's landmark for all who sailed out of the Mersey.

He had decided to make the Merchant Navy his career, but how to start had been the problem. He had written to the British Shipping Federation, the organization set up by the shipping companies through which seamen were signed on to their ships and through which the companies kept in touch with the general running of the service.

'Number eight dock, sir?' the old dockie replied in answer to Peter's enquiry. 'Go down Dock Road as far as you can and it's the far gate on the left, first before the container berth.'

'Thanks,' Peter said shyly, surprised at the friendly reply. The elderly man was of the old school and still possessed respect for a company's uniform.

At Hull, the principles of safety at sea had been drilled into the new cadets: the risks that were part of a seafarer's life; how to look after the seamen who would come under his supervision; general ship knowledge, life-saving, firefighting and accident prevention; basic seamanship and, finally, how a young man should look after himself and his health. It had been a good course and one which had whetted his appetite to join his first ship.

Peter had to admit that he had squandered his chances at school: too much fun and games and too little work had resulted in only three 'O' levels but, mercifully, they had been the right ones for the Merchant Navy: Maths, English Language and Geography. (He had just failed Physics which would have qualified instead of Maths.) With these qualifications, the O.N.C. seemed the best entry.

If he had worked harder at school he might have earned another 'O' level or two and perhaps even an 'A' — he could then have applied for the O.N.D. scheme, which was the most direct avenue these days to Command: four 'O's and one 'A' could have led him into the Nautical Degree Course and that was the surest path along which to become captain of one's own ship. Peter knew now that there was nothing which would bring him more satisfaction in life than the pride of eventually commanding his own vessel.

The first step was to have his eyes tested by the local oculist, a procedure which had to be arranged through his family doctor. 'It would be heartbreaking,' his father had said, 'if, after passing all your interviews, you were found to be colour-blind. Let's make sure first.'

That hurdle surmounted, the British Shipping Federation had been kindness itself in helping him with the entry regulations. For a 'deck' man there were four methods of entry: as a deck rating; as a deck cadet through one of the three schemes — the Ordinary National Certificate (O.N.C.), the Ordinary National Diploma (O.N.D.), and the Degree Course. All these schemes led eventually to the second mate's certificate (four years for a Rating Entry, three years for a Cadet Entry).

Even if Peter had not possessed his three 'O' levels, he could still achieve his ambition by entering the Gravesend Sea School for Pre-Sea Training as a Junior Deck Rating because he had been within the upper age limit of 17¼ years.

At Gravesend also were the boys training for the Catering Department, a vital component of the merchant fleet. Boys keen on engineering or radio had their own schemes of entry, the engineers spending four to five years ashore at workshop training, and the radio cadet officers, two years at a marine radio school. Both specializations could start at sixteen years of age, immediately after leaving school.

With Peter's limited number of 'O' levels, the O.N.C. seemed the best entry: he was lucky in having enjoyed Maths and General Science because one of these subjects was compulsory for entry qualifications. Armed with all this information the next step had been to find a shipping company that would accept him as a prospective cadet.

It had taken three weeks before he was fully equipped with uniform, a procedure which caused much mirth between his father and himself. Peter smiled to himself as he strode along the pavement of Dock Road, grip in one hand, raincoat over his shoulder. He moved aside for a girl walking towards him and he returned the smile of approval which she flashed at him: perhaps this newfound smartness was worthwhile, after all.

There was number eight gate: he could make out the entrance now, where those articulated lorries were turning off this busy road. He reached the gate and from out of the police hut stepped a constable not much older than Peter.

'Yes, sir, can I help you?'

Peter tried not to betray his embarrassment at this unusual form of address: the uniform again, he supposed, but the arm of the law was courtesy itself.

'Yes, sir. *Exmouth Haven*'s in number sixty-two berth.' He pointed towards a row of massive wharves and sheds, the jibs of the cranes towering motionless, like sentries, on the far side of the warehouses. 'Joining for the first time, are you? First ship?'

The policeman's friendly smile steadied the sinking feeling in Peter's stomach. He nodded and tried to grin.

'Good luck, then,' the policeman said, stepping out into the road. 'Reckon you'll need it in that old tub: there's always something going on in *Exmouth Haven*.' He pursed his mouth and, with a half shake of his head, turned to direct the driver of a lorry which had clattered up behind them.

Peter walked on between the warehouses of numbers eight and nine docks: to the right was a massive cold store outside which a queue of refrigerated lorries waited to unload. Peter glimpsed, for the first time, the buff tops of two masts. At the yardarm of the foremast, there streamed in the breeze the flag of the Haven Shipping Company — here she must be, his first ship.

The entrance to the warehouse opened into a neon-lit cavern bustling with life: lorries slowly ground their way to the loading bays; others waited to complete their loads from the endless belts transporting the cargo of meat carcases which debouched from the ship lying alongside. Peter approached two men deep in conversation: one was a dockie holding a checkboard, the other was a hatchet-faced seaman in his late twenties.

'*Exmouth Haven*?' Peter asked.

'That's her, the old cow,' the seaman growled. 'You the new cadet?'

Peter nodded. The seaman turned away and smirked at the checker. 'I'll be seein' you,' the man said. 'I'm the senior quartermaster.'

Peter felt dispirited by his first encounter with an *Exmouth Haven* man. Shrugging off the disappointment, he dodged beneath the net hanging below the conveyor belt which rumbled overhead, and picked his way between packing cases, wires and crane tracks to the dock wall alongside which lay his first ship. He looked up at the black wall towering above him like a castle; the hull of this general cargo carrier, refrigerated for the New Zealand run, was streaked by red blotches of rust where the paint had chipped and where the welding lines ran between the plates.

His eyes swept along her length, all five-hundred-and-twenty-feet of her, to the sheer of her bows curving away from his sight. Her upperworks and bridge were a dirty buff and her funnel, brown-streaked where the sirens leaked, sat squarely amidships, a weather-beaten mid-blue with a black top. Immediately above him, the samson posts of the working derricks reared, the wires to the winches slapping and swinging to the unloading rhythm. Peter hurried towards the lower grating of the companionway. He swallowed and began the long climb upwards, his eyes firmly fixed on the steps of the ladder until he reached the gangway some thirty-four feet above the water.

He looked up and crossed the gangway. As he set foot, for the first time, on the deck of *Exmouth Haven* he heard a man coming up behind him.

'Hullo, Pete.'

Peter Sinclair swung round. The voice was familiar and there, dressed in blue overalls and wearing a green pom-pom woollen cap, was Ned Hindacre. Peter was struck immediately at the change in him: the youth had become a man, the rounded face already hardened by long hours of peering into the winds and the mists.

'Ned — it's great to see you.'

Peter put down his bag and they shook hands. Ned picked up Peter's grip and began to lead for'd, along the port side of the upper deck.

'I'll take you to the chief officer,' Ned said quietly, his face bare of emotion. 'He's known as the mate,' and without further word, he leaned against the spring-loaded mahogany door which opened inwards. He waited for Peter to cross the combing of the door and pass into the athwartships passage which ran around the main stairway. Amidships was an office and over it a tally, 'Chief Officer'.

Ned put down his grip. 'I knew it was you,' he said. 'Bit of luck you coming.' He winked and replaced his gloves. 'See you later. Must go now or the bosun'll be after me.'

In the centre of the door facing Peter, gilt letters announced: 'Knock and Enter.' Peter tapped on the mahogany and gingerly pushed open the door.

A burly figure was crouched over a desk. Massive shoulders and a white shirt slowly heaved round and, from the desk, the face of the chief officer, the second-in-command, confronted him. Kindly eyes gazed serenely at Peter, dark brown and steady, like a spaniel's; a pudgy nose, like a boxer's, surmounted a wide mouth through which flashed a row of teeth. The roundness of the face was framed by a red beard, a forest of hair that twisted and curled round the side of his face, over his ears and up to his head which, strangely, was close-cropped.

'Welcome on board, Mr Sinclair,' the thirty-year-old officer said. 'My name's Pounder, Ralph Pounder, and I'm the mate.'

He indicated a chair by the side of his desk. As Peter settled himself on the edge, the chief officer hauled his huge bulk from the desk and, plucking his reefer jacket from a hook on the bulkhead, he donned it and reached for his cap. The man was enormous, at least six-foot-four, Peter thought, but he seemed lithe on his feet.

'You've arrived just in time, Mr Sinclair. You've got today to "sling your hammock" and tomorrow I expect you on duty. You'll be understudying the navigating officer but watchkeeping with Mr Blair. You'll be responsible to me for your college correspondence work and for seeing that your Record Book is properly kept and up to date. Bring it to me every month for signature.' He slapped on his cap and pushed through the door. 'You'd better meet Mr Nock; he's the chief steward.'

So, after meeting Hubert Nock, a dour-faced man with rimless spectacles who combined the duties of chief catering officer with those of chief steward, Peter was allotted his cabin; number 17 was two decks down and he was to share it with an engineer cadet, Dick Malin.

Peter took off his cap and sat down in the battered chair at one end of the space that ran between the two bunks. Malin's chest and bunk were neatly squared off and there was an air of orderliness about the cabin. When Peter leaned over to unzip his bag, he noticed a piece of notepaper lying on the coverlet of his bunk.

'Welcome on board,' he read. 'I heard you were coming but I am working on the steering engine until lunch — see you then.' It was signed 'Dick Malin — Engineer's Dogsbody.'

Peter smiled. That was better — someone with warmth, after all. He'd met a somewhat frosty reception or was it that everyone he'd met so far was concealing something from him? He squared his shoulders, a feeling of apprehension taking hold of him. He'd soon know: someone was bound to talk. He was halfway through his unpacking when there was a tap on the door before it opened.

A steward was standing there and he was grinning: 'Better look slippy. The Old Man's calling for you.'

Peter felt again the sinking in his stomach: like going in to bat, first wicket down. He grabbed his cap and glanced at himself in the mirror over the handbasin. His face had drained of colour and he looked weary about the eyes.

'For Pete's sake, get a move on,' the steward was yelling down the passage. 'He doesn't like being kept waiting.'

Peter rushed down the passage: the journey for'd and up the central stairway seemed endless but then, gathering himself together, he knocked on the door of the master's cabin.

CHAPTER 3: THE BLUE PETER

Captain Collingwood Kinane, M.B.E., was a dapper man, with short hair brushed back from his forehead. His features were like the rest of him, finely chiselled, even to the faint curl at the corners of his mouth. His pursed lips were small and compressed like those of a man seasoned by the discipline of duty. Below the twin rows of medal ribbons, a white handkerchief sprouted from his breast pocket. White cuffs protruded from his sleeves and the hand that wielded the thin-barrelled fountain pen was unusually small, the fingers long and sensitive. Peter stood motionless and at attention; finally he twitched at his tie in the hope that the action might stir this silent man to notice him, but the pen still continued to flourish the master's signature while Peter's eyes began to wander around the cabin.

The master's quarters were spacious. Prints of various *Havens* decorated the cream bulkheads and, in a frame on the other side of the door, was a photograph of *Worcester*, the training ship of earlier days. Below it was a row of hooks from which hung the captain's bridge coat, cap and binoculars. In the centre of the starboard bulkhead a curtained doorway led off to Captain Kinane's harbour cabin. A soft voice, pedantic and precise, brought up Peter with a round turn:

'So you're Mr Sinclair, eh?' The questioning eyes that stared at Peter were blue, pale and searching.

'What made you join my ship, eh, Mister Sinclair?' Peter could feel this man's gaze gliding over him, from head to toe. He felt uncomfortable and barely recognized his own voice when replying to the question which had been put with such peculiar truculence. Peter could hardly admit that he had applied first to the Port Line.

'I wanted to go deep-sea, sir, for experience in refrigerated ships and general cargo work.' He met the ice-cold eyes peering up at him, held them and did not flinch. His answer seemed convincing enough.

Captain Kinane paused, the ghost of a smile at the corner of his mouth.

'You'll certainly find all the work you're looking for,' he said. 'As to the rest, we've got a job to do and, as one of my officers, I'll thank you to pay strict attention to my orders and to persevere with your studies for second mate.' He paused momentarily, then sprung up from his chair. 'As long as you do your best to accept the high standards of discipline which I set in my ship, you'll get on well with me—' and he swung round to face Peter. 'But if you're slovenly or lazy, I'll see that you don't suffer long from that complaint. D'ye understand?' Again that bleak gaze transfixed the young cadet.

'Yes, sir.'

'My chief officer, Mr Pounder, will see to your studies which you are to keep up to date with Plymouth Nautical School.' He paused and thrust his hands deeper into his reefer pockets, his thumbs hooked outside. 'You must get to know this ship, every nut and bolt of her. I'll be inspecting your Record Book every month and if there's no progress or keenness shown, I'll discharge you when we return home. Neither I nor the company can waste time on loafers.'

Captain Kinane seemed an efficiency maniac, but there must be other ways, Peter thought, *of running a ship. At least the master of this ship was king of his castle.*

'The passengers will be joining tomorrow; there's no need to remind you that I expect punctilious good manners and every effort made to see that the voyage is a happy one in all respects.'

Peter nodded, tongue-tied by this ordeal.

'Any questions, Mr Sinclair?'

'None, sir, thank you.'

'That will be all then.' Captain Kinane turned away, but suddenly recalling a forgotten fact, he spoke with bitterness. He was staring through the for'd ports of his cabin to the well deck where the deck party were closing the hatches on number one hold.

'We sail on Thursday, the day after tomorrow. I'm always short-handed in this ship, but even one cadet can pull his weight. I asked the owners for three, but they sent only you—' He gazed at Peter again, disappointed at what he saw. 'They've promised to send another out to me as soon as an O.N.D. man can be found. Until then, you'll be on your own, except for the Engineer Cadets.' He turned to Peter. 'Met any of 'em yet?'

'No, sir, but I'm sharing a cabin with Malin.'

'Ask him anything you want to know. He's been with me nearly a year now. The ship's engines are nearly played out, so you'll not see much of him.'

He lapsed into silence and gazed moodily through the for'd ports. The meeting was at an end. Peter left the presence silently and sighed with relief when he gained the flat outside. He wouldn't cross the Old Man if he could help it.

'What made you join this ship?' This was the second time that Peter had been asked the same question but, lying on his bunk and listening to Dick Malin on the other side of the cabin, he began to feel an uneasiness questing at the back of his mind.

Malin was a plump, jolly youth with a round face and merry brown eyes that reflected an enjoyment of life. He had been kind to Peter and taken him round the ship, from stem to stern, and introduced him to the crew. Malin seemed pleased at Peter's arrival and now they were yawning and trying to stay awake in spite of the weariness they each felt after the long day.

'It's always like this before an ocean voyage,' Dick was saying. 'In a ship like this old tub, everything in the engine room seems to break down at the last minute and we can't get the parts in time. The chief has ordered us to work all round the clock: we sail the day after tomorrow.'

Peter liked Malin: his was a warm personality and Peter felt immediately that in this rotund and genial young man he had found a genuine ally.

'It's difficult to pinpoint but there's something strange about this ship, isn't there, Dick?'

Malin was lying on his back, his arms crossed beneath his head, as he stared up at the deckhead above him.

'She's an old ship,' he murmured sleepily, 'commanded by a master of the old school. She must be one of the last of the traditional cargo fleet and she's seen many years of service under this Old Man.' He paused and, when Peter had switched off his own bunk light, the engineer cadet seemed to be selecting his words very carefully:

'It's almost as if the old girl and the Old Man shared some secret: they've been together longer than any of us and neither of 'em will change their ways, whatever the rest of the Service does. Methods of man-management may change, but not for the Old Man: he believes in old-fashioned discipline and who's to say, in the end, that he's not right?' Dick was talking to himself and Peter was beginning to understand the relationship between a seafarer and his ship.

'Is the captain supported in his ideas?' Peter asked. 'Presumably his way of running things produces an efficient ship?'

'Certainly, *Exmouth Haven*'s efficient up to a point,' and Dick Malin paused again, carefully choosing his words. 'But the master has a continuous fight on his hands. The bosun, Paddy Mooney, is due for retirement too but, though he and the Old Man detest each other as men, they respect each other as seamen: when there's trouble they stand shoulder to shoulder against all-comers.'

'Is she a happy ship?'

In the long silence, Peter could hear the muffled exhaust of the ventilation system and could feel the tremor on the bulkhead behind his head from the pounding of the electrical generator in the engine room.

'How can a ship be happy if there's a curse on her?' Dick replied sleepily. 'That's what the old hands in the Indian crew believe: there's been a hoodoo on her ever since her maiden voyage twenty-nine years ago. Some trouble in New Guinea they say, when a tribal chief cursed the ship. It's all nonsense, of course,' Dick said, a long yawn punctuating his soliloquy. 'But it makes you think, you know, some of the things...'

Peter felt his own senses slipping into a stream of half-consciousness. Dick's voice seemed distant, murmuring in a dying monotone.

'Tomorrow's our last day,' Dick was saying. 'You'll see for yourself: there's still time for her to live up to her reputation.'

Peter was left much to himself on the next day, Wednesday, for all was bustle and hurry. Last minute stores arriving; the final race against time of the cargo loading; signing on the crew and the reception of the nine passengers; the final details of the passage plan carried out by the navigating officer, Charles Tussok; the frenzied efforts of the engine room personnel to complete the defect lists before sailing: all these and a myriad of other duties precluded any attention being bestowed upon the new cadet.

M.V. *Exmouth Haven* displaced 9,000 tons and, at full load, had a waterline length of 480 feet; with a length of 520 feet overall, she drew 62 feet. She was a refrigerated cargo-carrying ship who carried up to twelve passengers in special passenger accommodation built around the bridge structure. These passengers were usually bound for New Zealand and Australia but, sometimes, when on her homeward voyage, she would take passengers to ports in the East Indies and the China Seas if she was working those areas.

During the forenoon coffee break, a tall officer in his early twenties came up to Peter.

'I'm Harry Hicks, the fourth officer,' he said, a curl of amusement at the corners of his mouth. 'The mate has bounced me to take you on: the blind leading the blind,' he said, a dark-haired man, with a lean face and black, laughing eyes. He plopped his cap on the back of his head and swaggered out into the passage. 'As long as you don't mould yourself on me, Sinclair, you'll be all right. Come on, let's start for'd.'

Hicks threaded his way along the upper deck, past number one and number two holds and up the starboard ladder to the fo'c'sle head. He demonstrated the cable leads and the operation of both windlasses.

So it was that Peter made his first rounds of the ship, with Hicks pointing out the details of the deck fittings and the derricks. Peter was introduced to Magun Das, the deck serang, a bewhiskered Indian in a red turban who was in charge of the

Indian crew. His second-in-command was the deck tindal, Gokal Bhoj, a green turbaned Muslim, whose position corresponded to that of a bosun's mate. 'Bodger', he was called — and not for nothing, as Peter was to discover.

'Who does the serang come under?' he asked.

'The bo'sun, who in turn takes his orders direct from the chief officer. Paddy Mooney is the oldest bo'sun in the Company — he ran away to sea. One day Paddy will get going and yarn about his youth and his old mother: he's still terrified of her though she's ninety.'

Hicks turned about and began to walk aft along the upper deck when, from behind the superstructure at the after end of the bridge, there emerged a gnarled, rugged man in dark blue serge trousers, a dark green donkeyman's jacket and a red pom-pom knitted cap that sat squarely on his head. Below the narrow forehead jutted gingery eyebrows, and two sky-blue eyes were coolly appraising the new youngster standing before him.

'This 'ere our new cadet, sir?' Paddy Mooney asked. To the fourth officer's nod, the old bo'sun thrust out a hand as big as a ham which Peter took. He retaliated the bear-like squeeze with a grip of his own and the bo'sun grunted his approval. The wise old head, bristling white where the close-cropped hair sprouted from the parchment skull, jerked towards number two hold. The rectangular void yawned below him as Peter leaned over the steel combing to peer into the vast cavern three decks below.

'We're just finishing, sir,' the bo'sun reported. 'The lower and upper 'tween deck hatchboards won't be shipped for a while yet: I've got to clean the hold first.'

'MacGregor's going on now?' Hicks asked.

'Almost ready,' the bo'sun replied, nodding towards the vertical steel leaves of the MacGregor hatches which, concertina-like, were stacked up neatly before being swung across the hold by the derrick. Paddy Mooney glanced at the young cadet. 'Ye'll have to learn about safety, my lad, the easy way, before an accident teaches you the hard way. See that MacGregor hatch? Wonderful development but still mighty dangerous. Take my tip: never stand under a weight,' and he instinctively moved away from the boom which was swinging across to plumb the hatch covers. The bo'sun nodded and Hicks continued aft with his tour of the upper deck.

'We'll have boat drill tomorrow,' Hicks said, 'as soon as we leave the Mersey. They're pretty old boats but they float,' and, grinning, Hicks tapped the side of the huge steel lifeboat that loomed above their heads. 'They are supposed to run down the skids, even when the ship has a list of twelve degrees. With the crew, and most of them new for each voyage, boat drill is important.' He laughed with the assurance of experience. 'You'll see tomorrow, when you muster the passengers at boat stations.'

Peter began to feel the excitement of this new life, a strange quickening of his senses as the real nature of a seafarer's life was borne in upon him. The lives of the men, women and children could possibly lie in his hands one dark, tempestuous night. He must know how to turn out a boat in the pitch blackness; how to load the boat with passengers at the rail; and, in a heaving sea and with the ship rolling heavily, how to slip the lifeboat from its falls. He had to know every nut and bolt of his ship, and exercise thoroughly the various emergency drills.

Hicks scuttled down the ladder to the after well deck where the massive steel girth of the mainmast sprang upwards from between numbers three and four holds. The deck party were still working on number four but number three was battened down and covered with tarpaulin. On top, its weight distributed by huge baulks of timber, lay a gigantic phosphor-bronze propeller, its four knife-like blades protected by strips of timber. It was secured by a network of rope, chains and bottlescrews.

'Looks precarious, doesn't it?' Hicks said. 'Hope the mate has done his homework on stability. This old tub rolls like a basket at the best of times and this sort of topweight won't help.'

Peter grinned as he recognized the winchman operating the starboard winch of number four hold: Ned Hindacre grinned back, his eyes momentarily leaving the derrick and wires which his winch was working. On the port side, the senior of the four quartermasters was operating the hoist; Ned's momentary inattention had caused the port winchman to misjudge the lowering of the hatch which he was lowering into place. Down below in the hold was the cargo of cars, bumper to bumper and all securely lashed.

'For — sake,' the ginger-haired man on the port winch yelled across, 'Can't yer bleedin' well watch what yer doin'?'

'That's Rouse,' Hicks muttered as soon as they had passed the hatch combing, 'the senior quartermaster. He's too big for his boots.' He climbed the ladder to the poop deck and, standing beneath the red ensign which was fouled round the ensign staff, he turned towards Peter. With a sweeping gesture of his hands, he indicated the whole length of the ship stretching away from them.

'There she is, Sinclair. The oldest ship of the Haven Line: with the worst reputation, an old cow, with a bolshie crew and a madman for a master, we ought to have a good voyage. But I wouldn't swap her, no, not even for that beauty over there,' and he pointed across to the opposite side and to the other end of the dock.

'There you have a fine ship,' he added, '*Port Chalmers*: Port Line, one of our best companies. She's efficient, she's reasonably new, refrigerated like us and she's even on the same run — but I wouldn't swap her for this old girl—' and he stroked with affection the grubby handrail that ran round the stern. 'You never know what's going to happen next on board this hooker,' he said. 'Unlike *Port Chalmers* where everything goes like clockwork.'

In the afternoon, Peter was duty cadet on the gangway. A taxi drew up on the wharf and out clambered the first passengers, a middle-aged couple.

'Please give them a hand with their bags,' Peter said to the quartermaster, able seaman Ivor Rouse, a man of twenty-nine. The seaman, dark-haired, his face a closed book, was the same man who had yelled at Ned Hindacre that morning. He grunted and moved nimbly down the ladder, while Peter remained at the top.

'Doctor and Mrs Blair,' the jolly, round-faced man announced when he had reached the top step.

'Welcome on board, sir,' Peter said as he took Mrs Blair by the arm. She smiled, a quiet, efficient-looking woman with honey-blonde hair. Peter escorted the first two passengers and handed them over to the chief steward. Peter had carried out his first duty as a cadet on board *Exmouth Haven*.

The senior quartermaster gave a half-smile when Peter returned to the gangway. 'Enjoy that, did you, sir?' The tone was sarcastic. 'Your first job as an officer?'

Peter was at a loss. Able seaman Ivor Rouse seemed an unfriendly cove but Peter was saved from replying by the banging of another taxi door at the foot of the gangway. There was bustle and commotion while the family Gatewhistle, garlanded by brown-paper parcels and plastic shopping bags, clambered upwards: first, a ginger-haired boy, George, seven years old; then his sister Carol, about five, cherubic of face, with laughing blue eyes and red curls.

A fragile little lady of about fifty-five arrived next. She was wearing a grey coat and skirt, a grey pillbox hat perched squarely atop her greying auburn hair which coiled above her birdlike face. She stopped when she reached the deck and turned to await her sister, a broad-bosomed female with several chins and a brow-beaten air.

'We're the Dacres,' the wispy one said. 'We're coming with you to New Zealand. This is Miss Esme Dacre, and she nodded gracefully towards her voluminous sister, 'and I am Miss Juanita Dacre.' She inclined her head and the audience was at an end.

'This way, please,' and Peter led the last of the passengers towards the office. *An unpromising lot*, he thought, *with not a young person amongst them*. Mrs Gatewhistle was below thirty but she was a dead loss. Thank goodness the ship was picking up other passengers later on. Henry Deering, with an eye always on the main chance, had persuaded the second steward to allow him a sight of the passenger list. A family was joining after Sydney and amongst them was a Miss P. Withycombe whose date of birth confirmed that she must be eighteen. 'Hope springs eternal,' Henry had muttered but now, Peter reckoned, eternity would seem a short time.

Further aft, the bo'sun was talking to the chief officer who was pacing slowly up and down the wooden deck. The conversation continued for some time and then, to Peter's surprise, the chief officer beckoned him. 'Keep an eye on the gangway,' Peter said to the senior quartermaster.

'Aye, aye, sir.'

Peter doubled aft along the deck and saluted. The bo'sun, Paddy Mooney, stood respectfully behind the chief officer, out of earshot and inspecting closely the tackles of the port number four derrick.

'There's a spot of bother for'd, Sinclair. I want you to come with me as a witness. Bo'sun,' and the chief officer hailed Paddy Mooney whose face, a study of sheepish unconcern, suddenly brightened. 'I'll need you later,' Pounder said. 'Be in the offing.'

Peter followed the chief officer to the crew's quarters, a block of cabins arranged in a rectangle directly below the bridge. The mate walked in silence, his face grim as his eyes absorbed the cabin numbers and the names on the doors. 'Amar', 'Salim', 'Mobarek', Peter read. 'Randhir', 'Ahar', and 'Dantawit'. Outside this last door Pounder stopped, paused; he knocked and, hearing a shuffle, quickly turned the handle. He pushed open the door and entered.

CHAPTER 4: DEEP SEA

Peter peered over the massive shoulders of the chief officer who blocked the doorway. Two females were sitting at each end of the bunk. They were half dressed and Peter could smell the alcoholic fumes as the befuddled Indian in the middle staggered towards the door.

'Get 'em out of here,' chief officer Pounder snapped. 'And report to the serang.' He turned abruptly, nearly knocking Peter down.

'I won't have stowaways in my ship, Dantawit, and you know it.'

The cabin door slammed shut, the crash reverberating down the passage. Pounder was muttering over his shoulder at Peter as they climbed the companionway back to the chief officer's cabin.

'Find the bo'sun and tell him to report to me.'

The last day before sailing had begun inauspiciously. The bo'sun had overheard two of the quartermasters whose conversation had made him suspect that 'Twit', as Dantawit, the deck cassab, was good-humouredly known, had smuggled on board two women stowaways. Paddy Mooney, not wishing to upset Magun Das, the deck serang, had reported his suspicions to the chief officer, to whom the bo'sun was directly responsible. Magun Das, intelligent and sensitive of his position as 'boss' of the deckhands, had already announced in no uncertain terms to the chief officer that the bo'sun should first have approached the deck serang; Magun Das considered that Paddy Mooney had gone behind his back to the chief officer.

When the bo'sun told the deck serang that he wanted number two hold battened down and secured for sea, Paddy Mooney had received a surly and highly expressive grunt of disapproval. The deckhands, even Peter could see, went sullenly about their work, in silence and with gaze averted.

Thursday dawned at last for Peter. At 0830 the tugs appeared in the basin, one on *Exmouth Haven*'s starboard bow, one standing by amidships to haul off from the wharf and one aft beneath the counter.

Peter was detailed to understudy the navigating officer, the second officer, Charles Tussok. A man of twenty-seven, he was lean, dark and quietly efficient. Determined to earn early promotion (he had recently married), he was studying for his extra master's certificate. Success would ensure that the Company would notice his progress and perhaps consider him for command of one of their smaller 'rock-dodgers', a fleet of coastal ships who tramped round the British Isles and continental ports.

Tussok had been helpful and friendly towards Peter. He had explained the mysteries of his navigation department and had given Peter the job of chart correcting — a never-ending task that was to keep Peter up for many a long night in the future.

'Ring on main engines.'

Captain Collingwood Kinane had arrived on his bridge. The officer of the watch, George Blum, the third officer, moved swiftly to the telegraph indicator on the port side of the wheelhouse. He swung the handle from 'full-ahead' to 'full-astern' and then back to 'stop'. An answering jangle announced that the engine room was standing by: *Exmouth Haven* was ready for sea.

The pilot had arrived at 0800; the dock crane swung the last brow away from the ship and the deck party two decks below began securing the cumbersome gangway.

'Ready when you are, pilot,' Captain Kinane said from the port wing of his bridge. 'Haul down the house flag, Mr Sinclair.'

From the upper conning position, where the halyards of the Pilot Flag and Blue Peter were secured, Peter could see the length of the ship. *Exmouth Haven*'s passengers had breakfasted early and were excitedly lining the rails as the old ship gently moved away from the wharf. To the accompaniment of the pilot's whistle and the answering 'toot-toots' from the tugs' sirens, the wire hawsers were slipped from the bollards by the unberthing party ashore. A splash as the eyes of the wires flopped into the water; the whine of the winches as the wires were hove in and gradually the black, oily-scummed water appeared between the ship's side and number eight berth.

As the tugs took charge, controlled now by the pilot using his radio telephone, the massive bulk of nearly ten thousand tons slowly moved out of her river dock. In the restricted place outside the dock gate, the tugs began to turn her at rest, a lengthy evolution during which Peter, now awaiting orders from the navigating officer, was able to watch the array of ships of all nations gathered in this section of Liverpool docks.

As *Exmouth Haven* moved slowly ahead, the dock gates opened: a queue of bicycles and cars soon built up and Peter could see one or two waving hands, well-wishers of the ship that moved past so slowly with Blue Peter flying.

The gulls began to mew and cry, circling and wheeling above the ship as she bit into the swirling waters of the ebbing Mersey. Abreast the dock entrance she turned, moved swiftly down on the tide. On the jetty, the port control signal tower changed its coloured signals; the tugs slipped their hawsers, swirled under the bows and counter and, as suddenly, were rapidly being left astern as *Exmouth Haven* gathered way.

The chunking of the diesels now shook the funnel, its grimy blue plating visibly trembling. A green wreck buoy swirled past the port side and then, a few minutes later, a *Clan* boat moved swiftly past, trying to beat the tide.

C.22 light float next, its red upperworks marking the port north side of the channel, careered wildly in the fast-running ebb; a couple of dredgers lay ahead, barely visible in the low-lying fog that was clamping down.

'Start the hooter, Mr Blum.'

The visibility had shut down and fog lookouts had been placed. The radar aerial revolved above them to the accompaniment of its whining motor. In the wheelhouse, the plan position indicators (P.P.I.s) of the radars glowed in the fading light, the revolving sweeps being fingers of reassurance when navigating in these congested waters.

Two hours later the fog lifted. Away to the south-east stretched the hills of Wales, purple and blue as the last rays of the sun kissed the mountain peaks. To the north, sheer against the towering clouds of night, was the Isle of Man, now fast disappearing on the starboard quarter.

It was on the fourth day out, with the Azores a hundred miles to the south-eastward, that the Marconigram arrived: charterers required the ship to proceed to Barbados, there to pick up a cargo of sea-island cotton, a load that would fill number two hold. The charter was subject to a satisfactory survey of the hold and the surveyors would be on board as soon as the ship anchored in Bridgetown.

'All right, bo'sun?' enquired the chief officer. 'Let me know when you've cleaned out number two.'

'We never got a chance, sir, in Liverpool, after that breakdown on the transporter. There's still a lot of rice and wool about.'

It was unlike Mooney to make excuses and the chief officer took him up on it.

'What's the trouble?' he asked. 'Haven't you settled things with the serang yet?'

The grizzled white head shook sadly as Mooney stroked his chin, ruminating on the imponderables of life.

'Don't like to say, sir, only…' and he hesitated. 'But the serang's got it in for me after that deck cassab business.'

'Dantawit — and the women?'

'Yes, sir — and Twit's, sorry sir, Dantawit's work is no better. Scruffy, idle, and we can never find anything.'

'Have you told the serang?'

There was a pause as the old bo'sun considered once again his loyalties.

'Yes, sir, but it don't do much good after that stowaway effort.'

The chief officer was becoming restive and he brusquely told his bo'sun that it was up to him to run his deckhands efficiently.

'Let me know when the holds are ready for inspection,' he concluded, the interview at an end.

Peter was on watch during the afternoon, understudying Charles Tussok, the second officer. The weather had become sub-tropical, the decks hot underfoot; the sea sparkled and was very blue. Ploughing through the Atlantic Ocean, the ship pitched gently in the long swell.

Peter watched the flying fish, gliding effortlessly across the bow, parallel with the ship and dipping along the swell; curvetting and twisting above the turquoise sea, they would fly for hundreds of yards, inches above the water, until they splashed back into the ocean whence they had sprung. The master was, as usual, aloof and staring ahead at the horizon when the chief officer came up behind him.

'May I have a word with you, sir?' He saluted and Captain Kinane turned:

'What is it now, Mr Pounder?'

The chief officer, Peter could see, seemed embarrassed, hesitating to raise a delicate matter.

'It's inter-departmental trouble, sir, and I think you should know about it.'

'Go on.' Captain Kinane turned away, irritated by yet another domestic squabble.

'The passengers are complaining about the domestic water service, sir. Some of the shower pipes are permanently blocked and there are leaks in some of the pipe joints in the cabins. It's the same in the crew's quarters, sir: the bo'sun and the serang have both complained to the chief steward.'

The master turned upon his chief officer, and Peter could see contempt in the eyes of the arrogant old man.

'I thought you had that repaired in Liverpool, Mr Pounder.'

'The job was not finished in time, sir. The agent said he'd arrange for it to be completed in Auckland.'

'Well, what are you doing about it?'

'The laundry is affected too, sir. Apart from the delays with the passengers' washing, the engine room staff are complaining that they aren't getting their clean overalls back quickly enough. The chief catering officer is blaming the laundryman, sir, but it isn't really the poor chap's fault.'

'Whose fault is it, then?'

'The first engineer's, sir. The machinery is his responsibility. The C.C.O. has already been on to him, but the "First" says he's got more than enough to do already to keep the ship running than to keep on wasting time on an old system that should have been renewed years ago.'

'Why isn't the chief engineer doing something about it?'

'He's flat out on the defective compressor, sir: says the first's job is to maintain the auxiliary machinery.'

Captain Kinane could sense that there was urgency in his chief officer's report. With luck, with tolerance on all sides, the crisis would pass.

'Keep an eye on things, Mr Pounder. Your job is to run the ship internally and to see the crew is content.'

Exasperated, Pounder was about to continue, when he thought better of it. He saluted and disappeared into the chart room. Peter followed, for it was time to take the barometer readings. As he bent over the instrument, he overheard the mate and Tussok conversing in low tones:

'He doesn't realize the tension down below, Charles. What with the stowaway business, and now the fresh water fiasco, Magun Das and his boys are determined to get old Paddy Mooney.'

CHAPTER 5: CAUSE FOR ENQUIRY

It was during the early part of the forenoon watch on the tenth morning out of Liverpool that the low-lying smudge of Barbados was first sighted by Peter Sinclair. He was now understudying George Blum and he tried to keep the excitement out of his voice as he reported the landfall: the echo had already appeared on the P.P.I. but, to Peter, the first sighting was an unforgettable moment. He could smell distinctly the scent of land. Less than a minute later, as the master came on to the bridge to verify the sighting, the chief officer strode quickly into the wheelhouse. His face was tense and he spoke rapidly as he saluted Captain Kinane.

'Accident, sir: number two hold. The bo'sun has just reported and I'm on my way down now.'

'Very good, Mr Pounder,' Captain Kinane acknowledged, his eyes hard. 'What were they doing on number two hold?'

'Cleaning it out, sir, ready for the survey.' Pounder turned impatiently to the cadet. 'Nip down and ask Doctor Blair for his help. Bring him straight to the hold.'

Peter put down his binoculars and hurried from the bridge. He scurried down the ladders of two decks and quickly reached number five cabin, the Blairs' suite, where he tapped on the door. The door opened and there stood the doctor, lather half removed from one side of his face and clad only in his blue pyjama trousers.

'Chief officer's compliments, sir,' Peter said, 'but could you come quickly? There's been an accident.'

Doctor Blair nodded, wiped the soap from his face and slipped on his red dressing gown. Peter hurried on down to the next deck, the slip-slopping of the doctor's footsteps close behind him. Peter felt fear inside him: what horror was he going to have to face? Would he be able to cope? He had never seen a serious accident. His heart was racing as he pushed open the screen door which led into the well deck of number two hold.

A group of silent men were gathered by the hatch. The MacGregor was closed, but two men were lowering another lighting cluster through the 'tween deck opening. From the darkness below Peter could hear hollow shouting from the bo'sun and the serang.

'Make way for the doctor,' Peter said. 'Put a line on him.'

The pallor of the deck tindal's face, as he slipped a bowline around the shoulders of the silent doctor, boded the worst. Peter could see the light of torch beams flickering at the bottom of the hold, two decks and sixty feet below.

'Follow me, sir,' Peter said. 'I'll drop down ahead of you.' He turned to the deck tindal who was busy paying out the turns of the heaving line. 'Lower away, Bhoj.'

Peter dropped down into the trunkway, the sweating rungs of the steel ladder slippery in his hands. He waited for the red slippered feet above him to begin their descent and then he clambered downwards into the darkness.

He quickly reached the upper 'tween deck where he leaned back to feel the deck combing against him. The slow pitching of the ship was decreasing now: the mate must have asked the Old Man to reduce speed. Peter pushed aside the lowering line of the light cluster and continued with his descent down into the lower 'tween deck where he noticed several of the hatchboards were out of position. He knew then how the accident must have occurred — and he realized only too well how little chance a man would have, if he fell from here down to the steel ship's bottom some forty feet below. Peter forced himself on downwards to the torch beams flashing up towards him.

'For God's sake hurry,' Pounder's voice boomed in the empty hold. 'Have you got the doctor, Sinclair?'

Then, as Peter's feet touched the deck at the bottom of the ladder, the cluster suddenly spilled with a brilliant glare. In the pool of light lay a crumpled body and it was very still.

Not even death could interfere with *Exmouth Haven*'s programme. As soon as her anchor splashed into the waters of Bridgetown harbour, the charterer's surveyor scrambled up the gangway, hard on the heels of the medical officer of health. When the hatches of number two hold were opened, the surveyor began his inspection.

A different scene was being enacted in the master's cabin where the port medical officer of health and superintendent of police were making preliminary enquiries. Captain Kinane, the chief officer and Doctor Blair were seated with the two officials while Peter stood behind the doctor's chair.

The dead man was the unfortunate deck cassab, Dantawit. His body had been found by the serang who, with the deck tindal, Gokal Bhoj, had been searching for the missing man after one of the seamen, Hari Ghar, had reported that Dantawit was missing. Hari, an intelligent Hindu seaman, had gone to look for a light cluster while Dantawit opened up the steel doors to the trunkway between the well deck and the 'tween deck. There was no trunkway to the lower hold but only a ladder bracketed to the after bulkhead. When Hari returned with the light cluster, the steel doors were open but there was no sign of Dantawit.

Hari had clambered down to the lower 'tween deck and there seen the displaced hatchboards. He had approached these gingerly and shouted down into the darkness for Dantawit. He became alarmed when there was no reply and so he had hurried to find the serang. He had bumped first into the bo'sun who immediately organised the search party down into the hold. The serang had joined the bo'sun and they had both together found the dead body of the deck cassab.

'There's no more to be done,' the police inspector had said. 'We'll take the body ashore and arrange the funeral. What religion is he, Captain?'

The master glanced at his chief officer:

'Muslim,' he said and Peter saw Pounder nod his head imperceptibly.

'Cause of death, next of kin…' the port medical officer was murmuring as he filled in the death certificate. 'Most unfortunate accident…'

'There'll have to be an official enquiry I'm afraid, sir,' the police inspector said. 'But well not hold you up here as there's no suspicion of foul play, is there?'

'Of course not,' Captain Kinane snapped. 'My ship must sail tonight.'

Pounder, Peter noted, remained silent and, when they had all given their evidence, the meeting was declared at an end: an official winding up of the case would be held in Balboa. Peter went up top to the upper deck to clear his thoughts; as he reached the boat deck, the body of the dead man, covered by a red ensign, was lowered over the side in a Neil Robinson stretcher to the police launch below. The derricks loading number two hold remained motionless for a few moments, as Dantawit left his ship for the last time. Then they swung again, in a frenzy of activity as if to shut out the memory.

Number two hold was filled with sea-island cotton, huge bales of it, in record time. The MacGregor hatch cover was finally secured and the crew called to stations. The cable rattled down the navel pipe as the anchor came home. The old ship swung to port, under way again and bound for Colon, the port at the northern extremity of the Panama Canal. *At least, I'll get ashore there*, Peter thought, *though I saw nothing of Barbados except for the green patchwork of the banana plantations.*

On the third day out, the heat at midday had become unendurable. The ship was sailing through an ashen sea, an ocean without a ripple as far as the horizon. The only breeze was that made by the ship's speed: 'wind-scoops' had been rigged in all scuttles, but the passengers and those off-watch were sleeping on deck because there was little air in the cabins.

They passed Cartagena, the capital of Colombia, during the evening. The lights of the town were twinkling away to the southward as Peter came again on watch.

As they were crossing Francis Drake's last resting place, Nombre de Dios, with Colon but four hours distant in steaming time, the lack of fresh water brought tempers to flashpoint. The passengers had complained to Hubert Nock, the chief catering officer, about the quality of the food. He had stormed into the chief engineer's office to confront him with a blunt accusation:

'Look here, chief, your blokes are turning off the steam to my galley — and usually at mealtimes. It only happens when Clarke and Atkins are on watch.'

Chief engineer Angus Adamson was not the most tolerant of men at the best of times. Today he was trying to remain alert after being up all night in the engine room supervising the stripping down of one of the compressors. He had never liked the fussy chief steward and this outburst was typical.

'Can't blame them, Nock,' the chief said. 'You don't return their laundry. Dammit man,' and his Scottish sing-song suddenly became granite, 'in this heat a man needs a couple of shirts a day. If you manned the plates in this heat you'd need clean overalls,' and the chief stared hard and long at Nock.

'What are you going to do about it, that's all I want to know?' Nock was white with anger, his upper lip trembling.

'Do about it, man?' Angus Adamson roared, his sweating face flushing. 'Do about it? D'ye think I'm a ruddy magician? We can't take on any more defects until we can get spares.'

The two heads of departments were glaring at each other. Nock turned and swept out of the chief's cabin. By the time *Exmouth Haven* anchored off Colon that evening, news of the confrontation had run through the ship.

In cabin 17, Dick Malin was discussing the situation with Peter.

'Can you sense the atmosphere, Peter?' Dick was saying. 'The Old Man has stopped shore leave for the crew tonight. I overheard Rouse blinding away with the tindal.'

Peter was silent. One incident was following another and now there had been this fatal accident necessitating an enquiry — to be held by the British Consul tomorrow evening when the ship reached Balboa. Captain Kinane had made the mistake of failing to give a reason for stopping leave to the crew: he wanted them present and sober for tomorrow's enquiry.

CHAPTER 6: THE BIG OCEAN

At 0500 the next morning, *Exmouth Haven* weighed and, shepherded by sleepy tugs, was nudged into the entry to the canal in Limon Bay; by 0630, she was in the Gatun Lock. The level of the Pacific Ocean at the western end of the Panama Canal is some eighty-five feet below that of the Atlantic but, paradoxically, a ship is taken upwards by the Gatun Locks to the level of the Gatun Lake, before being dropped in two stages down to the Pacific. Peter looked over the port bridge wing to watch the activity on the lock-side: the 'mules', double-ended towing engines which ran on tracks along the lock, handled the ship's wires with the utmost dexterity.

Each lock was protected by an emergency gate and a safety arrangement of chains which could bring up in seventy feet a 10,000-ton ship moving at four knots. Should a vessel pierce one of these locks a major disaster would ensue, with the release to the lower levels of billions of tons of water.

After clearing the locks, *Exmouth Haven* forged ahead, slicing her way at twelve knots through the Gatun Lake, a torrid stretch of water that narrowed to the islets between the overhanging crags leading to the Culebra Cut.

This causeway had been hacked through the hills by Ferdinand de Lesseps and his hordes of sweating labourers. The fearful difficulties: building the Gatun Dam with its 7,200-foot length and its 2,000-foot base-width; the torrential waters of the Chagres River; the thousands who died of malaria and yellow fever caused by the scourge of the mosquito; the politics — all these were overcome by the doggedness and skill of the French engineers.

Peter was amazed by the luxuriant tropical flora, the massive carpets of blue-grey and green smothering the hills and islands: *not surprising,* he thought, *when Balboa, surrounded by its lush hills at the Pacific end, sometimes had an annual rainfall of 400 inches.*

It was in a torrential downpour that *Exmouth Haven* finally secured alongside number sixteen jetty in Balboa at 1730 that evening. Hardly had the lines been secured than the car of the British Consul splashed along the jetty to stop at the ship's side, where the serang was supervising the lowering of the ladder.

The start on the following day, the first of the twenty-two-day voyage across the Pacific, was not propitious. Firstly, Captain Kinane had been made to look a fool at the enquiry, a master not in full control of his crew: two of the Indians, with a surfeit of cheap Panamanian beer in them, had run foul of the police and been thrown into jail for the night. One of them, Randhir, was a key witness, but had been absent when summoned by the board of enquiry. The delay of this lapse caused the displeasure of the court, a sentiment which was reflected in the official report. When *Exmouth Haven* finally proceeded to sea late that evening, most of the crew and officers decided that the bridge area was best given a wide berth.

Peter learnt much about the art of the navigator's skill during *Exmouth Haven*'s passage across the Pacific to New Zealand. The voyage along the Great Circle was to take twenty-two days to Auckland at the veteran's economical speed of fifteen knots. During the afternoon of the next day, the blur of Malpelo Island came up on the port beam. Taking his departure from the island, Tussok set a Great Circle course for the landfall off East Cape, North Island.

During the next three weeks at dawn and sunset, Peter stood by the navigating officer, to assist with the star sights. On the third day out, they sighted the southernmost island of the Galapagos group, a disappointing grey smudge on the horizon.

'Can't see the attraction in the godforsaken islands,' Tussok said. 'But they still draw the treasure-seekers.' He was talking to himself in the wings of the bridge, glasses to his eyes, as Peter stood by to jot down the bearings into the navigator's notebook. 'There's supposed to be treasure buried in Isabela Island — Captain Kidd's, they say. Landslides have overwhelmed the favourite treasure trove of legend, so every expedition of repute now carries a diviner to locate the gold.' He turned and laughed at Peter.

A pleasant relationship developed between Peter and Charles Tussok who, though ten years older, seemed determined to give Peter a thorough grounding. Tussok helped the young cadet to complete his Record Book before Peter showed it once a month to the chief officer. 'I never had a scrap of help from anyone,' Charles Tussok muttered one morning. 'Might as well put it right with you, then,' he added, self-deprecatingly, as he checked Peter's sight working. 'If I can teach you, Sinclair, I can teach anyone.'

Men talk in the long watches of the night. Friendships are formed, opinions aired. It was during the morning after *Exmouth Haven* had crossed the line, on the second day out and a few hours before sighting the Galapagos, that Peter overheard subdued conversation between Tussok and Ralph Pounder, the mate.

The crew, it seemed, were seething with pent-up grievances. The heat of the tropics (the Crossing of the Line ceremony had been a dreadful flop, with no one's heart in the traditional arrival on board of the bearded King Neptune); and the canvas swimming bath rigged over number two hold added little to the joys of the passengers because it was continually monopolized by the shrieks of the Gatewhistle children. The domestic water supply was still working only fitfully, in spite of the half-hearted attempts of the second engineer to repair it. The result was still an inefficient laundry which, with bad rinsing of the clothes because of lack of water, caused Dhobi's itch to be endemic amongst all on board.

A serious source of grievance was the crass inefficiency of the new deck cassab, Mobarek, a Muslim and one of the older of the Indian crew. Not only was the fellow surly, but he could never be found and, therefore, was condemned as lazy. His gear was untidy and never in place; as a deck cassab he was a disaster. The deck serang had promoted Mobarek into the vacancy after the accident in number one hold, entirely because, the bo'sun said, he was a friend of Magun Das's and the job carried extra pay. Paddy Mooney would have selected one of the Hindus, Hari Ghar, an intelligent and keen young seaman anxious for advancement. The serang had been adamant and told Paddy that even if Mobarek was not selected, he would put forward the next Muslim's name, Randhir, the thirty-three-year-old who had crossed the master's tongue after the Balboa debacle.

The tindal was fomenting the discontent, the face of Gokal Bhoj a sly mask in the more remote corners of the ship: cabooses, storerooms, cabins where men could hide away and make trouble. Rouse, the senior quartermaster, championed Hari Ghar's cause, so the makings of conflict were only too assured.

'I'll be glad when we reach Bombay,' the mate said to Tussok on the fourth day out. 'The master has agreed to pay off the lot and sign on another crew.' His voice was low and, as he brushed past Peter in the charthouse, he said: 'Keep that to yourself, Sinclair, or I'll keel-haul you.'

Night followed day in repetitious monotony as *Exmouth Haven* ploughed her way westwards across the largest expanse of ocean in the world. The days became cooler and by the sixteenth day, as the ship left the Maria Theresa Reef to starboard, the canvas swimming bath was empty even of the Gatewhistles. Tropical rig was exchanged for blues and then, at dawn on the twenty-second day out, North Island's East Cape grew above the horizon, fine on the port bow.

Peter sniffed the air, excited by the first sighting, his nostrils picking up once more the scent of land, borne on the warm wind from offshore. Looking down from the bridge he could see small knots of seamen, the Muslims in several groups leaning over the ship's side and, peering westwards, the two Hindus by themselves.

'Just in time,' murmured Ralph Pounder to Charles Tussok. 'Hope the beer of Auckland does the trick.'

It was another thirteen hours before *Exmouth Haven* entered the Hauraki Gulf where Captain Kinane reduced speed. The night passage between the islands off Waiheke demanded a prudent mariner, so the master and Charles Tussok were on the bridge most of the night. Off Devonport, Peter lowered the jumping ladder for the pilot who, poised on the gunwale of the launch bobbing below, was waiting to clamber on board. The 'dockies' did not turn-to until seven which was the moment when the tugs nudged *Exmouth Haven* alongside number three berth in Auckland Harbour.

The next two days were hectic. A good run ashore helped to clear the air, and the subsequent loading and unloading of the cargo took men's minds off the trivialities of shipboard life. Rouse bullied his quartermasters, the serang chivied the hands, while Paddy Mooney quietly plodded along, methodically giving a good-humoured lead. The tindal and his men worked the winches from dawn to dusk, unloading the cars from number four hold and the sea-island cotton from one and two. The battens were rigged and then these holds were re-loaded with prime lamb carcases for the U.K. From now on, until returning to England, the cool-room would be running to capacity, for full refrigeration was required when plying the latitudes the ship was about to work.

Peter missed the passengers who disembarked at Auckland, particularly Doctor Blair and his wife who had made a point of finding Peter; as they shook hands Peter hoped that the astute doctor had not seen through the façade to sense the discontent 'tween decks. He watched the Blairs descend to the jetty below and he could not but regret that frustration with bureaucracy was the cause that had forced such a fine man to abandon his medical career in Britain.

Exmouth Haven sailed at dawn three days later and, passing between Three Kings Islands and North Cape, set course across the Tasman Sea for the four-day passage to Sydney. Passing beneath the colossal span of the great bridge, the ship secured alongside the big crane in Woolloomooloo, to offload the large propeller which had been carried atop number two hold.

Peter wandered aft to check the loading process. Rouse was on the winch, swinging in the cargo of tractors destined for Seoul in South Korea. The hatch covers were being secured with tarpaulins and the last four tractors were being dumped on top. Mobarek, as deck cassab, was lashing them down to eyebolts with chain and handy-billies. He went about his work sullenly, resentful of the extra demand put upon him.

'Shouldn't have these tractors on the hatch covers, sahib,' he complained. 'Ought to be all in the hold.' He kicked a hook into place, slapped a rolling hitch on the tackle and passed on to the next lashing. Peter checked the tackle and noticed that the hitch was with the lay of the rope and not against. Reticent at interfering with the experience of the cassab, he said nothing at first. Then, impelled by a sense of opting-out, he pointed out the error to Mobarek.

'It'll do, sahib,' the cassab said. 'For many years I've been at sea.' As he turned, Peter saw a sneer on the man's face: he was to regret that he had not underlined, more forcibly, the inadequacy of the deck cassab.

CHAPTER 7: A SEAMAN'S DILEMMA

It was seven months since she had left England before *Exmouth Haven* finally set course for Seoul. The old ship, with her capacity for general cargoes, was much in demand with the charterers and agents in the islands of Indonesia and the ports of the China Sea. The Indian crew, now within call of their own country, settled down and, in spite of the heat and erratic water supply, seemed resigned to the privations now that these conditions would not last much longer.

Exmouth Haven called first at Bangkok; next to the unhappy Saigon with its background of war; then back to Djakarta, Sourabaya and Makassar; through the Sumba Strait and down to Darwin. On her way back through the Lombok Strait to Balikpapan, a Marconigram ordered the ship to Seoul, finally to discharge the tractors before returning home via Singapore.

Peter could not believe that he had now been in *Exmouth Haven* for nearly seven months. The last six months amongst the islands of the East Indies had flown, every minute crammed with work and the fascination of this exotic corner of the world. Peter and Dick Malin explored the ports whenever they could snatch a few hours ashore from working the ship. Kalimantan (Borneo) and its beautiful girls, its carefree way of life and luscious vegetation, seemed a paradise.

Peter's work had progressed and he was now feeling more confident: Tussok was allowing him to take sights of his own and the mate had once congratulated Peter on the neatness of his Record Book. These had been the good days, but there was also the reverse side of the coin when Peter had not measured up. He had learned not to be too sensitive to admonishment, even when a rebuke was unfair. He had learned to accept a 'rocket', to forget it and to start again without resentment. He was enjoying life, glad to be free of the envy and malice of shore-side trade-unionism.

Then, on 5 August, the ship altered course for Seoul to leave Borneo to the westward by steaming up the Makassar Strait. Peter was taking his readings to complete his entries in the log; he entered the ship's noon position, 07° 02'N, 118° 58'E, which put her well in the Sulu Sea, 40 miles south-east of the island of Cagayan Sulu and 130 miles from the Balabac Strait at the northern tip of Borneo. He was surprised by the barometer reading: in four hours it had dropped nearly three quarters of an inch, from 30.50 inches to 29.68 inches. Peter peered again at the long tube, which now hung motionless in its gimbals, his eye, to eliminate parallax, at a level with the top of the mercury column. There was no mistake: the barometer was dropping fast. He was entering the reading when Fred Carter, their Sparks, hurried on to the bridge. His eyes flickered behind his spectacles, questing for the master.

'Where's the captain?' he snapped at Peter.

'Port wing.' Peter put down his pencil, surprised by Sparks's brusqueness. Carter was normally imperturbable, a dry-humoured man of twenty-six. He turned to the port wing of the bridge where Captain Kinane was trying to alleviate the discomforts of this dreadful heat. Clad only in his white shorts and sandals, he reclined in a cane chair in the only pool of shade cast by the bridge superstructure. He wore dark sunglasses and a battered panama hat which had seen better days. Carter stood by the chair and watched as Kinane digested the contents of the signal.

'Very good, Mr Carter. Be good enough to ask the chief officer to report to me.'

'Aye, aye, sir.'

Captain Kinane rose from the chair, his back glistening with perspiration. He strode into the wheelhouse where Tussok was handing over the watch to George Blum, the third officer.

'Mr Tussok, here's an imminent typhoon warning. Turn over your watch and join me at the chart table, please.'

'Sinclair,' Tussok whispered as he edged Peter from the chart table. 'Stick around in case you can help.'

Ralph Pounder hustled in through the after door, out of breath and buttoning up his shirt. His black eyebrows were raised in question.

'Typhoon warning,' Kinane repeated, his dividers pricking off distances from the chart. 'Rate of advance indicates that the eye of the storm should be over the Balabac Strait at midnight.'

The mate was wiping the sweat from his arms with a soggy handkerchief.

'I thought it was damned muggy,' he complained. 'The humidity is way up.'

Surrounded by his second-in-command and his navigating officer, Captain Kinane was driven to make up his mind. On his correct decision the lives of them all depended. He listened first to Tussok who advised cracking on at full speed to clear the Balabac Strait before the eye of the typhoon struck at midnight — in eleven hours' time. The path of the typhoon, he observed, was almost due west and, once the ship was through the strait, she could head up to the southward to gain shelter under the lee of the Kinabalu mountain range off the northwestern coast of North Kalimantan.

Ralph Pounder pointed out that Tussok's proposals depended entirely upon *Exmouth Haven* reaching the Balabac Strait on time and upon the rate of advance of the eye of the typhoon. If the Manila meteorologists' estimations were accurate, the ship would be in the lee of Balambangan island by the time the worst of the storm was upon them. If the weathermen underestimated the approach rate of the typhoon, it could engulf them with the Banguey and Malawali islands under their lee.

The alternative, as Captain Kinane pointed out, was to turn the ship immediately and to steam at full speed whence she had come this morning: back through the Sibutu Passage so that they could gain sea-room in the Celebes Sea before the storm struck. *Exmouth Haven* could heave-to there and ride out the typhoon. This course of action depended entirely upon how fast she could make an easting: if the typhoon burst upon them before midnight she would be trapped in the neck of the Sibutu Passage, with Cape Unsang immediately under their lee. This predicament could be even worse than the first alternative, but, at least, with the second choice, if the typhoon struck earlier, the ship could edge off into the Sulu Sea, because she would have made a good offing and be well up to windward.

'Hard-a-starboard,' Captain Kinane shouted to the helmsman. 'Navigator, what course to make the Sibutu Passage?' He picked up the engine room telephone and shouted down it for the chief engineer.

Tussok and the mate glanced at each other, Pounder shrugging his shoulders imperceptibly. The die was cast, so he had better secure the upper deck for heavy weather. He saluted his captain and left him shouting above the noise of the engine room telephone:

'Full speed, d'ye hear, chief? Yes, maybe for six hours.'

There was a pause and then Kinane banged the instrument back into its socket. His face was flushed and his mouth grimly set.

'Ring on full ahead, Mr Blum,' he barked. 'Revolutions for twenty knots.'

The rhythm of the diesels changed to an urgent vibration that shook the funnel casing and its guys. The log slowly crept upwards until its pointer was registering a fraction below twenty knots and there it stayed, steady.

'We've been too long out of dock,' Blum murmured. 'We could do with a clean bottom and that extra knot just now.'

'Steady on one-six-five,' Tussok said quietly to Blum. 'I'll tell the Old Man.'

Peter entered the alteration into the deck log and, before going below, he paused in the starboard wings of the bridge. Already the afternoon was unbearably muggy and a yellowy murk seemed to be shrouding the eastern horizon. He shivered in spite of the heat and ran quickly down the ladder towards the dining saloon. As he hurried along the upper deck, he passed groups of men already emerging from down below. Both watches had been called on deck and there was an urgency about their work as they secured the ship for heavy weather.

Peter could snatch only a few mouthfuls at lunch because the mate shouted at him through the door to buck up and check the lifeboats. By the time he again reached the upper deck (hardly fifteen minutes had elapsed), the wind was already singing in the rigging. The sea was whipping up, a sudden contrast to the lazy millpond it had been such a little time previously.

Peter checked the gripes, sweating up those on number three boat; he double-checked that the oars and gear were lashed across the thwarts, then he moved across to the port side to check the remainder of the boats. He searched for the chief officer and found him down in the after well deck, struggling with the bo'sun to secure some dozen twenty-gallon drums of detergent which, being volatile, were stowed, for fire and safety reasons, in the starboard after-corner of the well deck. The seamen were unravelling a long lashing and doubling it around the conglomeration of blue drums.

'Finish it off, Sinclair,' Pounder yelled above the rising wind, 'then join us aft. We've checked up, for'd.'

It was three minutes past seven before Pounder was satisfied. Every length of cordage from Mobarek's store had been commandeered and, down below, as well as from the upper deck, every movable object had been either placed on the deck where it could fall no further, or lashed. On the upper deck, the boom and derrick housings had been checked and double lashed by the serang and his men; the cable and the slips on the fo'c'sle were tightened up and handy-billies slapped on as preventers to stop the chain flailing about. The chief officer, taking Peter with him, clambered slowly up to the bridge again to report that all was secure.

The force of the wind startled Peter when he emerged through the windward screen door by the bridge ladder. The door was blown back, when it slammed with the crack of a pistol shot against the superstructure. Peter fought his way up the ladder to the bridge-wing where, for a moment, he turned his back against the wind to regain his breath.

The bridge clock indubitably claimed that the time was 1742: five hours after the imminent typhoon report. The old ship was battling into the seas which, by now, had risen considerably, whipped up by a wind force that had increased steadily the whole afternoon. A full gale was now blowing but *Exmouth Haven* was used to that. What sent a chill down Peter's sweating spine was not the strength of the gale but the yellow-tinged scud that stretched the whole extent of the eastern horizon. Above this dirty aura, huge banks of thick grey clouds billowed, swirling now and tumbling over themselves in strange confusion. The air hung heavily, a leaden band in the sky, hanging low, suffocating and threatening. The old ship was dipping into the swell, seas battering against her stern and now breaking green over her, to swirl away in her scuppers and slap against the bridge structure. Thumping into head seas like this, she would plunge down, stagger a moment, shiver throughout her length, then climb upwards again, out of the boiling troughs.

Peter entered the wheelhouse by clambering round to the lee side, the wind blowing so hard that he had difficulty in keeping his feet. Inside the wheelhouse was comparative calm, apart from the banging of the gusts against the bridge windows. The Captain, Harry Hicks the four-to-eight officer of the watch, and Tussok, were standing in silence, their faces against the windows, watching the mounting seas. The helmsman, wrestling with the wheel, steered calmly, his eyes never leaving the dancing compass card. Peter moved swiftly to the barometer. He could not believe his eyes: the mercury had plummeted downwards and was now reading 28.47. At that precise moment, the chief burst on to the bridge.

'I'll have to stop the starboard engine,' he said, confronting the master. 'The oil pressure's dropping and she's beginning to overheat at these revolutions.' Perspiration was running in rivulets down the oil-streaked cheeks of Angus Adamson. His eyes blazed anger, not only because of his captain's decision to overwork his diesels, but because he himself had been found wanting.

The master glared for a long moment at his chief engineer.

'Stop an engine, d'ye say, Mr Adamson? You can't stop it.' He paused a long moment, with a nod of his head towards the leaden skies outside. 'Not now, with sea-room within reach and only two hours ahead.'

'I've got to stop it, sir,' the chief said, 'or the whole issue will seize up. I'll let ye know when ye can have it again — if the damage is not too serious.' He turned on his heel without saluting and, shoving on his leather gloves, hurried out through the chart room door. Tussok had come up beside his captain. 'Shall I alter now, sir?' he asked. 'It's our only chance.'

Kinane nodded. The master's shoulders stooped and suddenly there was the look of an old man about him.

'Bring her around,' he said, 'before the chief stops the starboard engine. Steady her on three-four-o and make for the Balabac Strait.' He turned towards Peter. 'Warn them below that we'll be beam-on in a few moments.' Slowly he turned his back and, as Tussok brought the ship round, she began to roll heavily.

There was no need for comment from anyone on the bridge. All now knew that they would have to fight for survival. *Exmouth Haven* was in the worst of all hazards: a lee-shore under her and her only escape through a narrow channel six hours ahead which she would have to navigate on one engine at the height of a typhoon.

CHAPTER 8: THE TYPHOON

Cape Unsang disappeared astern as swiftly as it had emerged out of the murk. Now running before the gale, *Exmouth Haven* was making twelve knots even without a starboard engine. On the bridge, there was little conversation because all eyes were upon the helmsman.

With only the port propeller, the old ship was yawing badly, careering up to starboard in the troughs of the following seas. With the wheel hard-over to port, the quartermaster could barely prevent her broaching-to. She would roll dramatically, heel outwards, hang for a moment and then begin to claw up the mountain of water menacing the starboard quarter. Even with Rouse on the wheel, the ship was dangerously out of control at times. The quartermasters were taking one-hour tricks, the work being so exhausting.

'Cagayan Island, green five-o, sir.'

Tussok's report was like a pistol shot in the tension on the bridge. Captain Kinane's binoculars swept upwards and, as Peter looked, a blur, no more than a shadow poised above a foaming cauldron, swept down the starboard beam and into the murk on the quarter.

Tussok was bent over the bearing ring of the compass and, as he scrambled to the chart table, he collided with the master who was peering at the revolving trace of the sounding machine. The navigating officer's parallel ruler flickered across the chart, the pencil streaked and a small triangle appeared.

'Estimated position, here, sir,' he said. 'We must have passed between Cagayan and its off-lying island, without sighting it.'

'Agrees with the soundings,' Kinane snapped. 'Near one though, pilot.'

The ship was yawing badly when her bows failed to lift to the swell. A huge sea crashed against her starboard quarter, spinning her round, beam-on to a wall of water cascading down from astern. She swung swiftly, beam-on and hung there for a long moment, listing heavily to port.

'She won't answer her helm, sir,' the quartermaster shouted above the tumult. 'Wheel's hard-a-port, sir.'

Kinane had clambered round to the bridge windows, his face white in the gathering gloom of twilight. It was almost dark now, night falling much more swiftly with the advent of the racing low cloud.

'Full astern port,' he shouted. 'Wheel amidships.'

Ned Hindacre was on the wheel and his face was white. He seemed to be fighting the wheel, the veins of his bare forearms bulging with the effort. Then the compass card began to swing in the reverse direction, as the ship gathered steerage way again.

'Slow ahead port. Hard-a-port.'

Kinane was now coaxing her back but the navigator's face was tense as he crouched over the chart table.

'How much to allow for her sheer to windward?' he said in an aside to Peter. 'That's my difficulty.'

As if in answer to their unspoken thoughts, the master's summons dragged Peter back into the wheelhouse.

'We've got to have that starboard engine.' He turned to the cadet who stood before him, with his feet astride and clinging by his arms to the binnacle.

'I can't get any sense out of the engine room phone, Mr Sinclair. Go down and tell the chief engineer with my compliments, that if we're to get out of this I *must* have the starboard engine.' He glared at his cadet, then nodded in dismissal.

Peter saluted and slithered from the bridge. He decided not to risk the upper deck, so descended three decks to the passage leading to the engine room entry door. As he reached the lower level, the hull was like a tin biscuit box, drumming from the continual pounding of the seas. At each blow, the ship shivered and, as her stern reared upwards, the whole structure vibrated as the port propeller threshed clear of the water between the troughs of the seas. Peter reached the engine room door, wrenched it open and forced his way inside.

Peter slithered down the ladder to a group of men clustered round a pipe at the foot of the casing on the starboard engine. The chief did not notice the newcomer at first. The second engineer, a greaser and two engineer cadets were frantically trying to offer up a long length of wide bore steel piping but, in this heaving world, they were finding it impossible to hold the pipe in place. Wedged against any projection they could find, each man was making super-human efforts to hold the pipe steady long enough for 'the second' to slap on sufficient bolts. Then, just as the pipe was in place, the ship would fall away beneath them, list heavily and fling them against the protective rail of the port engine.

'Sir,' Peter shouted above the bedlam, 'the captain's compliments, but he says he's got to have the starboard engine if we're to get out of this.'

Angus Adamson wiped his oil-streaked face with a wad of cotton waste. He leaned wearily against the rail, his eyes gazing with professional interest at the length of steel piping. He smiled patiently at the cadet, sorry for the lad bearing such a provocative message, noting the tired face which had suddenly turned white, and with a green tinge at the base of the cheeks.

'Tell the Captain we're doing our best, son,' he shouted. 'Ask him to keep the ship steady and he can soon have his engine.' The chief smiled wanly and turned back to the job in hand. 'Mebbe a couple of hours.'

Peter felt ill, nausea sweeping over him in this heaving, oil-laden world. He could reach the upper deck in time, if he quit now. He turned and scrambled up the ladder, back to the world outside. He reached the port screen door on the upper deck of the bridge structure as the sickness hit him. He had had enough sense to choose the leeward side where he vomited for what seemed an eternity. In between the bouts of his sickness he watched the black seas hissing upwards at him as the ship listed over to meet them. He glanced at his watch and, even in his misery, he was surprised how the time, which had dragged so painfully since the first typhoon warning, had slipped by. It was now 2155 and, to his amazement, the wind seemed suddenly to have vanished. The seas still heaved, but those vicious breakers now seemed to have little power in them as they cascaded down the length of the ship's side. Peter pulled himself together and entering again the bridge structure, climbed back to the bridge. He had to repeat twice the message from the chief to the captain. Kinane swore beneath his breath, but spoke out loud for all to hear.

'This is the eye of the typhoon, gentlemen,' he said, his voice flat, a defeated man caught in something beyond his control. He was wiping the moisture from his face, the mugginess being overpoweringly oppressive. 'We've got about twenty miles of comparative calm while the eye passes over us.'

'Banguey Island is twenty miles ahead, sir,' Tussok said. 'It's just come up on the P.P.I.'

'Thank God,' Kinane muttered. 'We've a chance, if we go right through the centre of the eye.'

He prised himself from the corner of the port side of the bridge where he had been standing for the past hour, and hauled himself over to the radar screen. There, coming up right ahead, was a pinprick of light, a luminous speck denoting the right-hand edge of Banguey Island. Then, as they watched, the echo slowly faded. Kinane stood for a moment, staring at the dead screen. He thumped the visor with his fist. An alarm bell began clamouring from the corner of the bridge as the lights faded, then suddenly went out.

'Gyro's off the board, sir,' the helmsman shouted in the darkness. 'Compass card's stuck.'

The engine room telephone squealed from the bulkhead.

'Switch on emergency lighting,' Tussok commanded. 'Steer three-one-o, magnetic, quartermaster.'

'Three-one-o, magnetic, sir. Aye, aye, sir.' Peter sensed the authority of Charles's voice, a reassurance instilled by the decisiveness of Tussok's authority. The navigating officer had rushed to the chart table to check his magnetic course.

'Can't hear,' Captain Kinane was yelling above the sudden activity. 'I'll send the cadet down to you again, chief,' and the master snapped the phone back into its rest. 'The primary generator's run wild I think, Mr Sinclair. Nip down and report back the situation.'

As Peter reached the well deck, he heard the rain. It came with a roar, advancing like an express train, until they were suddenly engulfed by sheets of driving water. As swiftly, the wind swept hard upon the heels of the rain — giant gusts that laid the ship over. As the seas boiled around them, the glare from the light clusters in the aft well deck were suddenly dimmed. In the half-darkness, Peter glimpsed the marionette jerkings of the men struggling with the tractor lashings. At that instant, the full fury of the typhoon struck *Exmouth Haven.*

Peter stood transfixed. A wall of water sixty feet high towered above her starboard gunwales; the gigantic sea stretched across the horizon to shut out the sky. Peter grabbed a stanchion as he was flung against the rail by the shock wave that whipped throughout the length of the ship. The seas came up to meet him as her lee side went under. She was laid on her beam-ends, her side flat in the water.

An elemental power bore the ship down, down, until the plates groaned from the stress. Under water now, Peter felt his lungs bursting. Choking and gasping, he floundered for a handhold on the superstructure that was now a roof above his head. As he began to lose consciousness, the ship quaked, hung horizontally. Then, slowly at first, shuddering as she shook herself free from the mass of water, she began to right herself. She catapulted upright, then wallowed helplessly, deep in the troughs of the sea.

Above the roaring of the typhoon there was injected into Peter's consciousness another sound: the shouts of terrified men. He shook his head to clear his senses and, as he crawled to his knees, he gazed downwards at the well deck beneath him.

A jumble of tractors was piled into the port after corner: the securing tackles must have snapped like pack-thread when the ship was laid flat. The tractors were now loose, an uncontrolled mass of many tons which could move its collective centre of gravity with devastating speed across from one side of the ship to the other. Interspaced between the sheets of water cascading across the deck, the jerking glare from the light clusters cast shadows upon the scene.

The bo'sun was there, his calm authority taking charge of the emergency, his sturdy figure motionless in the centre, while the deck serang, the tindal and five or six seamen milled around him. The chief officer stood halfway up the well-deck ladder, the better to see the extent of the chaos. His face was frozen in horror as he pointed across the deck. All heads turned towards the stack of volatile detergent drums roped together on the starboard for'd corner of the well deck.

Peter scrambled down the after ladder to add his strength to the pitiful numbers stunned by the prospect of sudden disaster. Though the ship now lay with a port list and lower in the water, once more on her beam-ends, she would be flipped upright again so swiftly that the tractors would be shot across, a tangled mass of rasping metal, into the inflammable drums. The fire that would result, fanned by the wind, would be impossible to extinguish; the volatile chemical would engulf the midship section and incinerate the engine room crew below.

'Get a wire around those tractors,' Pounder was yelling through his cupped hands. 'Encircle them, bo'sun; it's our only chance.' The mate was tearing off his jacket to help; he splashed down into the water swilling about on the deck, determined to snap the terror-struck men into action.

'Come on, Sinclair. Let's get moving.'

Peter dashed after the rotund figure who was already grabbing at the end of the wire coiled around the port for'd winch. 'Take it, and secure it somewhere to the after screen.' As Peter grabbed the eye of the hook, Pounder slithered forward to release the brake.

Bhoj, the tindal, hung back, his face grey with fear. Mobarek, the deck cassab, stood by him awaiting orders. It was the young Hindu, Hari Ghar, who staggered forward to help Peter unreel the 1½-inch wire. Foot by foot, as they struggled in the water that was now up to their knees, the two men overhauled the wire until there was enough scope to snatch the hook to a deck ring bolt by the after screen. At least the wire now had a secure anchorage by which to encircle the tractors in the bight, if a hold-fast could only be found.

'Jump to it,' the bo'sun yelled at the terrified Indians who, awaiting their serang's order, were still motionless onlookers under the control of the tindal. 'If you want to live, for Pete's sake, *MOVE*,' he raged at the panic-stricken seamen. The serang, Magun Das, abandoning for once his dignity, strode forward in the water and grabbed the bight of the wire, shouting imprecations at the tindal.

It was Daniyal, the Muslim seaman, who moved first, the friend of Mobarek, upon whom Mobarek leaned so much for help. Daniyal shouted and jerked his head. The tindal and Mobarek followed, impelled into action by the realization of the fate which awaited them if the tractors gathered momentum again on the ship's next crazy roll. Peter felt the bight of the wire taking up as the five men on the other end began to haul away.

'Lift the wire, Sinclair,' Pounder screamed above the shrieking of the wind. 'As high as you can.'

Hari Ghar needed no prompting. Together, he and Peter began levering the wire upwards as the strain came on; inch by inch the wire bit deeper into the conglomeration of the machinery.

Pounder, in soaked shirtsleeves, was at the head of the bight. With Paddy Mooney, he waited for the precise moment to catch a turn around a cleat on the port for'd samson post. Waiting for that split second of stability at the bottom of a roll, the mate yelled at the hauling seamen.

'Stand by to come up...' He stared upwards at the starboard gunwale then shouted, '*now* — COME UP...'

Peter felt the tension suddenly slacken in the wire. He saw Pounder and the bo'sun flailing to catch the turn. Then, at that precise moment, a monster sea crashed into the starboard side of the ship. At that instant, too, when the disaster could have been averted, the deck cassab panicked as he glimpsed the mountain of water towering above them. He screamed, pointed upwards, and let go his grip on the wire. In that second, too, the ship, a void beneath her, flipped to starboard.

Peter, realizing what was happening, jumped aside, flattening himself against the ship's after screen. Mobarek, with no handhold, slipped; he fell prostrate and slithered into the centre of the hatch covers. The mass of tractors began to slide athwartships, slowly at first and then with gathering momentum.

It was Hari Ghar who first saw the danger. Whilst the others hung back, mesmerized by the impending tragedy, Ghar dashed forward to scramble across the flooded deck. With arms outstretched towards the aged Mobarek, he yelled as he bent downwards. The cassab glanced upwards; his eyes stared, pleading deliverance from the monsters now lumbering towards him.

Mobarek screamed. The tractors somersaulted. At that moment Pounder and the bo'sun caught the turn, doubled it and backed it up. The wire came taut, sang, trembled then held fast as the ship reached the bottom of the roll. The mass of red-painted machinery checked; the ship swung back and, with a rush, the load heaped back into its original corner. Peter rushed forward and grabbed the next bight and, in seconds, a second span was rove. When Peter looked up to collect himself he saw a silent knot of men bending over a motionless figure at their feet.

CHAPTER 9: THE REEFS

Mobarek was dead. The shock had caused cardiac failure. In the battle against the fury of the typhoon there was no time for formalities, and his body was covered and left in the shelter of the port passage.

Exmouth Haven was now at the mercy of the wind and the seas that raged about her. As the water gained remorselessly in her bilges, she began to settle lower in the troughs of the seas. The night dragged slowly onwards. At any moment, those on the bridge expected her to broach, her one engine being inadequate against the elemental forces that raged against her. Again and again she would swoop away to starboard, reeling sickeningly to port, as she slithered down, down into the deep abyss.

Rouse and Hindacre had now doubled up on the wheel; it was only their strength and immediate reaction to the sudden sheer which prevented her final over-setting by the seas.

Captain Kinane stood in the port bridge corner, his tired eyes glued to the starboard bow, watching the seas soaring above the starboard wings of the bridge. Then a messenger from the engine room staggered on to the bridge to report that the compressors were not keeping pace with the demand for H.P. air because of the continuous engine movements: the H.P. air in the reservoirs was running out. Once the air was exhausted, the engine could not be restarted. With no engine and no steerage way, the ship would founder at the first broach-to.

Peter knew that the greasers and engineer officers were fighting a losing battle under appalling conditions. The ship was now paying the price of her age. With her sinking, Peter's and fifty-six other lives would be snuffed out.

Even if the ship survived this battering; even if she saw the first light of dawn that seemed a lifetime away, she still had to pass safely through the Balabac Strait.

Suddenly Peter saw Tussok standing before him. His arm was outstretched, pointing; his mouth was working but no sound came from it.

A dark spectre boiled down their port side, a jagged pinnacle of rock. As swiftly as it appeared, it was gone — and, as they stood transfixed in unbelief, a shadow loomed suddenly, high above the heaving crests, a gigantic cliff, shapeless but, as it slid rapidly past them, overwhelmingly close.

'Malawali,' Tussok yelled towards the captain. 'It's Malawali, sir… We're passing between the islands.'

The face of the master was a mask. He gazed at Tussok, then continued to peer through the glass windows that ran with water. The shoulders shrugged and slumped back into resignation.

'Soundings confirm it, sir.' Tussok's face was white. 'Can't believe it; we've passed between the islands. Ruddy miracle.' He whispered the last words then continued, shouting aloud: 'At our rate of leeway we should be past Kudat in a couple of hours. If we don't land up on the cape; if we can round up to the southward, we'll be sheltered in the lee of the land.'

They had been spared being dashed to pieces on the Malawali Rocks, but if the ship could not turn to port, she would sheer up to starboard and broach-to before turning to the southward. If she failed to turn, only disaster awaited them: the notorious reefs, the Swallow, the Royal Charlotte and the Louisa, were lying right in the ship's path. They would be invisible in this foaming cauldron.

Two hours later *Exmouth Haven* succeeded in rounding up beneath the cliffs of North Borneo where she sheltered in the lee of Mount Kinabalu. There she licked her wounds, pumped out and re-stowed her gear before proceeding onwards to Malaya.

She limped into Singapore Roads, rust-splotched, battered, her upperworks and boats a shambles where mountainous seas had swept away every fitting. The tugs took her, nudged her into a repair berth; the agent ran up the gangway and within the hour, repair gangs, fitters, welders and riggers were swarming on board. *Exmouth Haven* spent nearly a fortnight in Singapore.

One of the first problems which swiftly forced itself upon the chief officer was Mobarek's successor. The deck serang, Magun Das, plumped strongly for Daniyal, Mobarek's only friend. The bo'sun's choice was Hari Ghar, the intelligent young Hindu. Mooney argued that, with someone as keen as Hari, neither the bo'sun nor the serang would need to chase and double-check as they had been forced to do in the past.

Ralph Pounder had little choice. The obvious man for the job was Hari Ghar and during the second afternoon in port, the young Hindu assumed the duties of deck cassab. The storm in the teacup seemed to be over.

The break in wireless communications during the typhoon had delayed the Marconigram which had been dispatched by the owners. It was somewhat of a surprise to the master to find, waiting on the jetty, the new cadet who had been sent out by air to join *Exmouth Haven* and appointed as the second cadet under training. Peter, who was busy at number one hold and helping the serang to check the cargo stowage, was dumbfounded to see his new 'opposite number.'

'Well, I'll be blowed,' Peter said, wiping the sweat from his forehead: 'Morgan Finnimore.'

Of all people, why did the Haven Line have to select Finnimore as the other cadet for *Exmouth*? Peter tried to hide the disappointment welling within him. The face with that sardonic smile was certainly Finnimore's. The large youth stood hands in pockets, with his back to the sun.

'Sinclair,' Finnimore drawled. 'Thought it must be you when they sent me out to this old tramp...' and the eyes lazily encompassed the rusty vessel from stem to stern in an appraisal of assumed contempt. 'See you...'

Peter returned to the hold, his thoughts in a whirl. The life with which he had come to terms would now lose its savour. Finnimore, the root cause of his unhappiness at the factory, was to be living cheek-by-jowl with him. Then Peter began to chuckle to himself — hell's bells, was he going to be got down by a man like Finnimore?

During the afternoon, the passengers for the United Kingdom arrived on board. Two families had joined: the Thompsons, with their two young sons; and the Plummers, an army family on its way home with Granny, Mum and the three prodigies between eight and three, again all boys. It was the tenth passenger who excited the interest of the ship's junior officers.

Peter, like the others, had learned to appreciate the charms of young women. Panama, New Zealand, Australia, the East Indies — all had their fair share of dollybirds. Who, therefore, could believe that fate could deal the cards so kindly when Penny Withycombe stepped on board *Exmouth Haven*?

She was an unusual girl. Eighteen years of age, she was tall, slight of figure and walked with the grace unique to the women of the East. She was an orphan. Her parents, Malayan rubber planters, had been murdered by the communists when she had been an infant. Brought up in a convent, she was now a student nurse and was on her way home to England to further her career in a London hospital.

The pallor of her oval face accentuated eyes that smouldered like coals beneath her wide forehead which was framed by her sleek, black hair which she tied with a red velvet bow at the nape of her neck. She was dressed simply in an open-necked shirt and linen skirt.

When she had appeared at the gangway, Finnimore had regrettably been 'duty boy'. From that first moment he made it plain that Miss Withycombe was his personal 'perk'. She had been in the same hotel in which he had been staying while waiting for *Exmouth Haven* to arrive in port — and, sniggered Morgan, they hadn't wasted much time getting to know one another.

During that first evening, Henry Deering suggested that they might like to see the night life of Singapore, so Finnimore, Penny Withycombe, the engineer cadets and Peter made up a party. Finnimore announced that Penny and he had seen all this before, but Peter found Chinatown both fascinating and disturbing. The squalor, the overcrowding of teeming humanity, the garish tinsel of the shops; all this and the poverty of evil-smelling back streets were counterbalanced by the vitality of these amazing people. They were Chinese, and would always be so, albeit in a foreign land. By their enterprise and industry they would always survive, a proud people with a dignity that befitted only patriots of a nation whose traditions emanated from the beginnings of human history.

It was the dope-bedevilled wrecks who shocked Peter most. Listless, with emaciated arms outstretched in supplication, the drug addicts lay in the gutters, ignored by the bustling passers-by who took them for granted as a fact of life.

'Horrifying, isn't it, Penny?' Peter muttered. 'Some of them so young, and dead already on their feet.' The girl, her arm in Finnimore's, looked up quickly. The dark eyes in her pale face seemed frightened and she turned away.

Morgan laughed shortly. 'It's their own damned fault,' he snapped. 'Shouldn't worry too much about them.'

Time slipped by, the working days followed by evening runs ashore. After a second foray as a combined party, Finnimore, being off-duty alternately with Peter, took Penny off on his own, which did not please the others. Then, on the Friday night, *Exmouth Haven* was finally secured for sea. The Blue Peter fluttered lazily in the airless night; in the morning, the tugs would be alongside at eight.

CHAPTER 10: A HUMAN TRAGEDY

The first of the monsoons had broken by the time that *Exmouth Haven* had cast off from the repair berth in Singapore. There was no one, amongst passengers and crew alike, who was not relieved to escape the humidity of Malaya and who did not anticipate with pleasure the weeks that lay ahead.

Hari Ghar's undoubted efficiency, though improving immensely the general running of the deck department, did not bring peace into the troubled crew's quarters. But with only one more port of call, Colombo, in which trouble could erupt, the ship's officers were beginning to feel that the worst of the tension might be over.

Passing through the Malacca Straits, *Exmouth Haven* had steamed for four days across the Indian Ocean. A day in Colombo to discharge a load of rubber, and to embark crates of carpets and boxes of tea, was as long as Captain Kinane would linger before proceeding on the last leg of the passage to Bombay — now a mere two-and-a-half days' steaming away.

For Peter, the only bright star in this oppressive atmosphere was the presence of Penny Withycombe. With her trim figure and neat, fresh clothes in this sultry weather, she seemed the only desirable asset on board the ship. Now that a long voyage stretched ahead, she had managed to elude somewhat the possessiveness of Morgan Finnimore. Now she shared her time with the rest of the younger officers, including even Cadet Sinclair amongst her court.

Peter was beginning the long hours of 'the middle' and he yawned as he watched Daniyal, the seaman of the watch, hanging about impatiently for Rouse who was late in relieving the eight-to-twelve quartermaster. Coffee cup in hand, the Indian was impatient at the delay and Peter went up to him and jocularly sympathized. Finnimore, whom Peter had relieved, had wasted no time in leaving the bridge.

The minutes dragged by, the interminable hours of the middle watch a test of anyone's endurance. To the northward, the distant steaming lights of a ship on opposite course slid down the starboard side. George Blum, the officer of the watch, had disappeared into the charthouse, leaving Peter to hold the weight. As Peter carried out his all-round lookout, he found his mind wandering once again to the uneasy questions which Finnimore's behaviour had prompted.

It was, Peter supposed, not unusual for a man of Finnimore's arrogance and conceit to try and monopolize the only pretty girl on board. His attitude was so possessive — and she so pliant — that it made anyone wonder how such an attractive girl could become so besotted by a man with such obvious failings as Finnimore's. Though he was an O.N.D. Deck Cadet (his was the degree course in Nautical Science lasting four years), he was not only loud-mouthed but his brashness and bounce surely concealed an inadequacy of which no one was aware. That pale, sly face framed by flaxen hair seemed unhealthy in its pallor. *Sour grapes*, Peter thought, *that's what the trouble is, just because he claims Penny's attentions and I can't...*

The ship's bell sounded 0200, rung by the seaman of the watch. Half the watch gone. Peter felt the heaviness on his eyelids. He longed for a full night's rest — that was something the landsmen could never realize, how unbroken sleep became a conscious craving in a seafarer's life. When he reached home, his father would understand if he 'crashed' for a full twenty-four hours' sleep. How far away his parent seemed, he and his unshakeable faith. Would he understand Finnimore? How would he deal with him?

Morgan was on Peter's mind again; the fellow was becoming an obsession, probably because there was a mysterious barrier about him which Peter was unable to penetrate. Only yesterday, the chief officer had rebuked Finnimore for his familiarity in dealing with the crew, and particularly with the tindal, Gokal Bhoj. *Absolutely deserved*, Peter thought: *if ever there was an unreliable character, it was Bhoj.* Peter had been surprised in Singapore when, on his own whilst snatching a moment to buy soap and toothpaste, he had found Finnimore in conversation with Gokal Bhoj in the Paradise Bar. They had not noticed Peter who had quietly departed, not wishing to be hauled into a round of drinks. Peter had wondered then, but he had kept the matter to himself and Ralph Pounder's rebuke had not come as a surprise. Finnimore had been in a foul temper yesterday — probably the result of the mate's rebuke. He, Finnimore, had no reason for his moodiness — he was an O.N.D. and Degree Course man, who had more time to do than Peter.

The watch crawled by, the ship pounding through the dark night, the stars obliterated by the low cloud of the monsoon. Peter stretched his legs by walking from one bridge wing to the other, each time passing the helmsman who, spokes of the wheel turning in his hands, kept his eyes glued to the compass card. The glow from the binnacle lit up the man's face but Rouse tonight preferred not to speak.

'Rounds, Sinclair; it's three o'clock.' Blum's voice boomed from the charthouse. 'I've got the weight — and don't forget my baccy.'

'Aye, aye, sir. Course three-three-o. Speed fifteen knots. No ships in sight; nothing on the radar.'

Peter slipped out of the charthouse door. At least fetching Blum's tobacco would be a break in the monotony. He'd nip below first and pick up the baccy before doing rounds of the upper deck and, by the time he reported back on bridge, another half-hour would have slipped by — 0330. Strange though, he had not heard three o'clock sounded on the ship's bell. Maybe he *had* dropped off for a second; it was unlike Daniyal to forget striking the hour. Peter slipped into Blum's cabin and picked up the tin of pipe tobacco and climbed to the upper deck. He'd start on the poop and work for'd up the starboard side which was in the lee. He shivered as the night air again hit him.

The ensign fluttered and flapped at the ensign staff, the wake stretching a pale finger into the darkness astern. He checked the lifebuoy, shut a screen door that someone had left open. He clattered down the ladder on to the after well deck, checked the boom and derrick lashings. Up again, to the midship section of the upper deck where the funnel pulsated above him, the roar of the engine room fans deafening all else. The gratings over the skylights shivered and through them Peter glimpsed the brightness of the lighting in the engine room below, a glaring contrast to the dark night and the shadows cast by the police lights that illuminated the main gangways on the upper deck.

As he moved out from behind a ventilator, he noticed an unusual shadow, elongated and swinging like a pendulum in rhythm with the roll of the ship. The dark shape was traversing the deck and, where it met the starboard screen, bent grotesquely upwards. Peter moved forward towards the for'd lifeboat until he was stopped in his tracks by the sight which confronted him.

Wrapped around the fore davit head was the bight of the boat's for'd lifeline. With meticulous care a sheepshank had been tied on the bight and from this, immediately below the davit head, there hung the limp body of a man. As Peter ran forward he knew that the staring eyes and the strangulated face belonged to Daniyal. Peter stopped and touched the hand that was half-outstretched, as if in supplication.

They buried him at sea. The shrouded corpse seemed so slight as it slipped from under the red ensign to slide with a splash into the ocean. The crew, which had gathered on the poop with Captain Kinane and the ship's officers off-watch, stood in silence as the wake enfolded the lonely man who had been unable to cope with life's vicissitudes. He had lost face when Hari Ghar had been promoted deck cassab above him: this disgrace he could not bear. The group of men dispersed and, still shocked by the tragedy, continued the day's routine as if nothing had happened.

On the next morning, Magun Das presented himself before the chief officer. He declared that the Muslim crew to a man blamed the bo'sun and the ship's officers for Daniyal's death. Did the chief officer intend speaking to the crew? Ralph Pounder retorted that he would address the company before paying off on the next morning, after going alongside in Bombay.

Thus it was that the crew was discharged, the whole company, except for Hari Ghar, filing silently down the gangway. As Magun Das's red turban was lost in the mingling of the native stevedores ashore, the man did not even turn round to wave. He represented his Muslims and he had turned his back.

'It was not their fault,' Ralph Pounder was heard to say, sighing with relief. 'I'm glad to see the last of 'em, but some were good hands.'

In the afternoon, a new crew was signed on, each man making his cross on the engagement form. Before disaffection could spread from ashore, *Exmouth Haven* sailed at dawn on the next day and set course to pass through the Mozambique Channel for Cape Town where she was to pick up mail.

Table Mountain was no disappointment to Peter, its grandeur a theatrical backdrop to the capital city of the Republic of South Africa. *Exmouth Haven* lay wallowing in the Bay waiting for the mails to come off, her officers leaning over the rail.

'Why can't it always be like this?' Ralph Pounder was saying. 'Everybody happy.' The thirteen-day passage from Bombay had been one of peaceful contentment.

No one answered him, too overwhelmed with wellbeing to recall the unhappy days of the past eleven months. This was what the merchant service was all about — hard work, a good crew with a common purpose: these essentials made a happy ship. Even Captain Kinane had regained his bounce and, with only the last lap ahead of them, a seventeen-day passage of 6,100 miles to Liverpool, they might even be home by Christmas. The clank of the cable coming home was music to the ears of the married officers and, as the ship swung to a northwesterly course, Peter felt for the first time the thrill of a homeward-bound passage.

The days soon became hotter, the nights more sultry. It was after dinner one night, as they were approaching the equator, that Peter sensed someone coming up behind him. He was leaning over the poop rail and watching the phosphorescence of the wake stretching astern like an arrow into the dark horizon.

'It's too hot to sleep,' a girl's voice murmured. 'D'you mind if I join you?'

Peter caught the fragile scent, felt the proximity of Penny Withycombe as she leaned on the poop rail next to him.

'Just finished the first watch,' Peter said. 'I'm trying to cool off before turning in.' He turned and smiled at her, welcoming her friendship. Peter wondered why Penny had sought him out: she seemed to be the life and soul of the party and had evinced little interest in the ship's youngest cadet. She spent so much time with Finnimore that Peter naturally fought shy of her. He liked her well enough, but her gaiety seemed brittle, as if she were not entirely at ease. There was a mysterious slant to her and Peter, up to now, could not fathom the girl.

She began with trivialities, discussing the day's activities, questioning Peter about his shipmates. Then, as the tension eased between them, Peter felt the barriers come down and she was herself at last, not trying to impress. Her mood had changed, and now she was asking about him, his life and hopes.

'You don't like Morgan, do you?' The abrupt query was a statement. In the silence that followed, she shyly placed her hand across his on the rail. As Peter searched for a suitable reply, they were both facing aft, staring at the wake that disappeared into the southern horizon.

'You needn't say any more,' she murmured. 'He told me you were friends once, in the factory.'

'He was always so much better than me at everything,' Peter said. 'He's a clever chap.'

She laughed shortly. 'Too damned clever by far.' She removed her hand. 'Wish sometimes I'd never met him,' she whispered.

'Why d'you say that?'

'Nothing.'

The rumble of the diesels seemed far away, the rushing of the waters beneath them encompassing their private world. Peter felt close to this girl and he wanted to share her worries. He put his arm about her shoulders, but he continued to stare into the darkness.

'Tell me,' he said. 'I'll help if I can.'

She was crying, he could feel her body trembling as she tried to control the sobs. The floodgates burst, the words a torrent that she could not contain. For fear of embarrassing her, Peter remained silent.

Events had proved too much for her. Morgan, she said, could be irresistible, particularly if he was determined on a conquest to which, in her case, she had willingly surrendered. She had fallen head over heels, for this was her first serious love affair after escaping from her childhood. They spent a deliriously happy week together, exploring the city and travelling into Johore where they picnicked on the edge of the jungle and swam in the rivers.

She had been infatuated by him and it was then that he introduced her to the drug scene. Little of Morgan's persuasion was needed for her to agree to their making easy money. He had explained to her that, if they were clever, they could make enough money out of smuggling a small packet of heroin back to Liverpool to set up for life together. It would be too easy.

She was weeping again and, as she sniffed, a little girl bewildered by the situation, she laid her head for comfort upon his shoulder. Peter felt the moisture of her tears through his tropical shirt and his heart went out to her as she poured out her story.

Morgan had, by then, so involved her, that she had acquiesced to his plan. She helped him to smuggle the stuff on board: less than five hundred grammes in a small package, but enough to raise a considerable sum from the peddlers. It had been Gokal Bhoj who had played the middleman, the shifty deck tindal with whom Finnimore had been consorting too familiarly. He had arranged the contacts with the peddlers ashore and Penny, at Morgan's insistence, had hidden the package in her cabin.

'What are you going to do?' Peter asked when she had calmed down. 'They could send you to prison.' He stroked her black hair, the tears on her cheeks wet in his hand.

'What can I do?' Her face turned upwards towards him, a pale almond in the glow of the stern light. 'I can't betray him, can I, Peter?'

'Go to the Captain,' Peter said. 'I'll arrange it for you. Tell him everything. It'll be all right providing you tell him now.'

'I can't, Peter.' She spoke violently. 'If I split on Morgan, he's going to tell the hospital authorities. That's what he said.'

'You wouldn't be accepted by the nursing school. It'd finish you.'

'What am I to do?'

Peter recoiled, astonished at her intensity.

'Give him back the heroin,' he advised. 'Tell Finnimore to do his own dirty work. He'll have to get it through the customs himself.'

She did not reply for a long moment. She nodded her head slowly, then, wiping her eyes, smiled up at him. She raised herself on her toes and gently placed her hands on his cheeks. She pulled his head down and kissed him gently on the lips.

'Thank you,' she whispered. 'Don't tell a soul, will you?'

Peter shook his head.

'Promise, Peter?'

'I promise.'

She turned then and was gone, her footsteps tip-tapping into the darkness as she ran for'd.

CHAPTER 11: PENDING FURTHER ENQUIRIES

At last, through the murk of a grimy December day, the grotesque bird perched on top of the Liver Building came in sight. The Liverpool tugs were there, waiting like sheepdogs where they nudged the tidal stream. Bustling and tooting their sirens, they shepherded *Exmouth Haven* through the locks and into number eight dock from which she had sailed eleven months ago.

'Ring off main engines.'

Captain Kinane slipped the straps of his binoculars over his head, nodded at the pilot and led the way below. Peter, excitement welling inside him at being home again, stowed the navigational instruments. He walked out to the bridge wing and looked down at the dockside below.

The gangway was already hoisted out, the quartermaster, Ned Hindacre, standing at the head of it, with Finnimore who was duty cadet for the day, officially taking charge of the evolution. On the dockside stood the usual groups of officials: the marine superintendent, the agents and the customs men. There was an extra knot of officials, two in mackintoshes who waited there; with them were twelve policemen, their blue uniforms and checkered caps making a strange contrast to the casualness of the other onlookers.

'Tell Finnimore to see that no one enters or leaves the ship.'

The chief officer had issued his orders and Peter was sent to deliver the message to Morgan Finnimore on the gangway. Thenceforward events developed into a nightmare for Penny Withycombe and, to a lesser degree, for Peter Sinclair who, two days later, left *Exmouth Haven* and the Haven Line for good.

Back at home, Peter recounted over the supper table the events of that day to his father. The grey-haired man listened attentively, allowing his son to tell his story in his own words.

'After noticing the police squad on the dockside,' Peter was saying, 'it crossed my mind that something odd was up. I felt certain that the police contingent must be a drug squad. I wanted to warn Penny. Had she really returned that package of heroin to Finnimore?'

'As I rushed below to find her, the passageways were already blocked by policemen who seemed to have the whole operation buttoned up. "What's your hurry, lad?" one policeman asked. Then I realized that my face and my haste must be betraying my anxiety. Anyway, Dad, I failed to find Penny in time because, just as I caught sight of her congregating with the others in the passengers' saloon, the mate sent me off with a message for the duty cadet. No one was to enter or leave the ship.

'Morgan Finnimore nodded his head when I found him on the gangway. He seemed normal enough, grinning that sardonic smile of his. I returned to the passengers' lounge where, once the bo'sun and the serang had made their reports that everyone was present, the senior detective told us why they were there. Drug-trafficking was suspected on board.

'We were all courteously informed of our rights in law because a thorough search of the ship had already started. Everyone was therefore entitled to be present when the cabins and personal gear were searched. The dogs were already on board to help sniff out the drugs.'

Peter Sinclair sat back in his chair, sipping his coffee. There was an angry gleam in his brown eyes, his jawline accentuating the stubborn streak in his nature.

'They searched the passengers and their cabins first. Nothing was found and I breathed with relief for Penny, because I suppose I was more fond of her than I realized. Then they started on the crew and the ship's officers, a procedure which took most of the day: even Captain Kinane was included.

'My turn came soon because Finnimore was on duty and would be searched last. Dick Malin, my engineer cadet friend and I stood about in our cabin like a couple of prunes while the detective searched our gear. He went through Malin's wardrobe and found nothing. The whole thing was a routine operation; we felt embarrassed and cracked some pretty feeble jokes.

'Outside was a dog-handler and, as the detective began rummaging through my chest of drawers, the Alsatian began yowling and tugging at his chain. The detective looked at me and beckoned in the dog-handler. In seconds, they found a small package tucked between a couple of my tropical shirts.'

The father rose from the table and, putting his arm about his son's shoulders, gently led him into the sitting-room where a log fire blazed. He pointed to a chair and, lighting his pipe again, threw Peter a cigar. Then, relaxing by the warmth of the fire, the son continued to recall the events of that disastrous day.

'I don't know whether they believed me or not,' he went on. 'But Penny was a brick and told them, in front of me, the whole story from A to Z. "It was a plant," she said. "Too obvious to be credible." So they sent a man up to fetch Finnimore down to my cabin.'

Peter shrugged his shoulders. 'You know the rest, Dad. Finnimore was not on the gangway. He'd sent the quartermaster off on a message and, when the man returned to the gangway, Finnimore had disappeared.'

'What's happened to him?' the older man asked, pressing on the bowl of his pipe with his thumb.

'Bolted. Just broke ship. He left all his gear on board but they reckoned he took half the heroin because Penny said that the package found in my cabin was smaller than when she had last seen it.'

'It's good to have you home,' his father said. 'But why did they let you go?'

'The police had no choice, Dad. I am obviously under suspicion, and so of course is Penny. She is guilty of an offence, even though she has confessed. The police are trying to find Finnimore, and Penny and I are bound over, pending further enquiries. We've been told that the case will be heard in a few weeks and that we should continue our normal working lives. The police hinted that we should keep quiet because, if we were telling the truth, Interpol might be able to root out the source from which the peddlers obtained their drugs — Singapore presumably.'

'Well, thanks for telling me. What are you going to do now?'

'Dunno,' Peter said as he scratched his head. 'I was grateful to the Old Man you know, Dad. He stood by me at the enquiry and told the police that he was certain of my innocence. He said afterwards that it would be better for all concerned if I found another ship for a short spell — something I'd decided to do anyway. He recommended tankers to me and said it would be good experience. What's your view?'

Thus it was that within days Peter was interviewed by a Training Officer of one of the nation's largest tanker-fleet operators: Pisces Tankers (U.K.) Limited. There were several vacancies amongst their ships but, as Peter was liable to be summoned at any time to defend himself in court, a short appointment would be more sensible.

'Captain Pelly was asking for another cadet,' the Training Officer said. 'How would you like a Lightening Tanker, Sinclair?'

Peter jumped at the opportunity: this was one of the crack jobs in the Merchant Navy, so he had heard. The 'lightener', a 'small' tanker of about 80,000 tons, would meet a Very Large Crude Carrier (V.L.C.C.) in the Channel and off-load enough oil to lighten the V.L.C.C. sufficiently to reduce her draught so that she could enter the shallower refinery berths.

'*Marlin* is lying at Thames Haven. Can you join her by noon tomorrow? She's sailing on the afternoon tide.'

Peter was already rising from his chair, a smile creasing his face. 'Thank you, sir, for giving me the chance. I'll catch her.'

'I'll telephone Captain Pelly.'

The Training Officer rose from his desk. 'Good luck, Sinclair,' he said. 'You'll make a "tanker" man yet,' and he smiled as he shook Peter by the hand.

CHAPTER 12: LIFEBLOOD OF THE NATION

Peter found it difficult to believe that he had arrived at Thames Haven. The forest of tanks and the slender chimneys flickering with flames, were they all real or was he still dreaming? The rush to collect his gear, buy new uniform and catch the train at Liverpool Street had been frantic, but at last he was here.

'What ship, sir?' demanded the security guard on the gate.

'*Marlin*.'

'Fine ship. Number seventeen berth.'

Peter paid off the taxi and stood for a moment at the bottom of the huge brow which stretched sixty feet upwards to the top of *Marlin*'s gunwale. He was suddenly overwhelmed by the contrast of his new ship and *Exmouth Haven*, who now seemed so remote and belonging to an age that was almost past.

The old ship had taught him much during his eleven months in her. He was no longer an overgrown youth without self-confidence or self-respect. He had learnt discipline the hard way, through the inflexible methods of Captain Kinane. Peter did not now regret his training. In spite of indifference from remote owners, the hard-working and devoted efforts of men like Tussok and Pounder had managed to weld an old ship into a workable entity. With unreliable machinery and out-of-date methods, they still kept the ship at sea: by their seamanship and persistence were able to survive the worst of the fury of the elements. Peter's regret at the manner of his leaving *Exmouth Haven* was matched by his eagerness to join this, his second ship, one of the most modern, medium-sized tankers in the world.

The Pisces Headquarters in London, with its flags fluttering proudly from the summit of its tower block, were a revelation. Inside that enormous complex, centrally heated with its own internal ventilation system, toiled and lived five thousand highly trained Pisces personnel. From here the daily transportation of eight million tons of oil was organized.

As Peter gazed up at *Marlin*, he felt a surge of satisfaction. This splendid ship represented all that was modern, all that was best in the Merchant Navy. Though one branch only of the service, the means by which these fine vessels were operated were fast replacing the methods used to run the older vessels like *Exmouth Haven*. He smiled to himself at her memory and began briskly to climb the long gangway, his suitcase and grip swinging by his sides as he went.

'Welcome on board.'

The greeting came from an officer in white overalls who, in protective gloves and carrying a wheel spanner, was supervising the singling-up of the mooring lines. He stood on the green-painted deck and his open face smiled. 'I'm one of the chief officers,' he explained. 'Philip Margesson. My better half, John Fairfax, is checking the fire mains. There are two mates in the lighteners,' and he laughed as he explained. 'V.I.P. treatment. We're not supposed to be overworked on this lightening job.'

A hose swung across them as the loading booms were swung back and then the dockside crane driver held up his thumb as a *Marlin* seaman hooked on the hoist to the brow.

'You're just in time,' Margesson added. 'We slip in half an hour.' He turned to a burly man of about twenty-eight, with fair hair and blue eyes who, though barely five foot, had enormous shoulders and who was as tough as they come.

'Chief petty officer, take over will you? We'll just nip up to the captain.'

Before Peter knew what had happened, he had been introduced to Captain William Fortescue Pelly. Chief officer Margesson had introduced him to the master who, in spite of the imminence of casting off, had received him with old-world courtesy.

'We'll get down to details later on, Mr Sinclair,' the tall man with thinning grey hair said quietly, as he buttoned up his reefer. 'I'm glad you have joined us, though it's only for a short spell.' He reached for his cap and moved towards the door. 'Come on the bridge where you can see what's going on. Mr Margesson will instruct you later in your duties.'

When *Marlin* slipped from the fuelling jetty at the Thames Haven terminal, the ebb had already begun to run. With two tugs ahead and with one astern, the great ship, now that she was in ballast and standing up high to present considerable windage, was surprisingly easy to haul off against the onshore breeze. Going ahead and astern on her single, huge propeller, she wiggled out from the two dolphins on the jetty. The pilot paced from one wing to another, chatting on the R/T to his tugs. He glanced up-river and then slipped them, thanking them as he did so.

Peter stood unobtrusively in one corner, amazed at the serene efficiency of the evolution. Captain Pelly stood in the port wings while she nudged free; then came into the wheelhouse where he watched, without interference, the conduct of the Trinity House pilot. *These men*, thought Peter, *were the salt of the earth.* Calm, masters at their trade, they manoeuvred the monsters of the shipping world, day in, night out — throughout the year — into the berths of all the tidal harbours of these Islands. With, at times, only eighteen inches under the keels of these vessels, the responsibilities on the shoulders of the pilots were immense. 'We don't often get a bad one,' Ralph Pounder had said and he should have known.

The bridge seemed, in Peter's eyes, like the foyer of a modern theatre. With the soft material of the deck-covering beneath their feet; with the green-tinted glass of the enclosed bridge; with the subdued corrections and reports from the navigating officer, Esmond Hully; and with the monotone acknowledgements of the quartermaster, the atmosphere was one of supreme professional competence. Peter felt a surge of pride, an intense sense of purpose at being now a member of this elite company.

Marlin was now moving over to the starboard side of the channel in the lower reaches of Old Father Thames. At seven knots she was under complete control and, now that the anchors and cables were secured for sea, the sea-dutymen were set. Ships, large and small, plugged past. With only her special Thames lights denoting that she was a ship of unusual size and therefore difficult to manoeuvre, *Marlin* soon left astern the lights of the refinery, twinkling in the night like a forest of illuminated Christmas trees.

The ship slid down the Thames until she reached Sheerness at the mouth of the Medway. The Isle of Sheppey and then the rising downs of Kent, sloping towards North Foreland, came up next, as the ship began to thread through the channels of the Thames Estuary. The Yantlet, and then she was clear of the shallows, heading for the open sea. The downs of North Foreland sloped upwards to their crown, whence the beam of the lighthouse had begun to steal across the sea at the base of the cliffs. Evening twilight, on this December day, was barely distinguishable from the dour afternoon and, with a long night ahead of them, the ship's company had settled into seagoing routine.

Peter had a spacious cabin to himself on the port side of the bridge deck; the other cadet, John Platt, a pleasant youth, round of face and freckly, was in an identical cabin on the starboard side. Platt made the newcomer welcome but turned in early as he had the middle watch. Peter unpacked his gear in silence and, weary after the past hectic forty-eight hours, stretched himself out in the clean linen of his bunk. He sighed with contentment at the prospect of a spell in this superb ship. Tomorrow he would explore her and begin a new life as a tanker officer.

The dawn was unusually soft for December. The sun climbed slowly into the eastern sky, the pale orb concealed by a bank of fog that stretched across the horizon astern of them. Tinged by the pink sunrise, the bank slowly dispersed to allow the warmth of the winter sun to filter through the chill of the early morning. As Peter waited on the upper deck outside the door to the chief officer's quarters, he watched the blue and purple of the shadows, scudding across the Isle of Wight, a changing kaleidoscope of colour where the sun chased the clouds. Culver Cliff fell away to the northward, while Dunnose and St Catherine's Point grew larger and more distinct with every minute that passed.

'Come in, Sinclair.' Chief officer Margesson's breezy voice summoned Peter into the office where a fair-haired giant leaned against the bulkhead, holding out his hand.

'I'm the other chief officer,' he grinned. 'John Fairfax. I look after the cadets.'

So it was that Peter was detailed his duties and, to acquaint him with the geography of the ship, he was to act as assistant to chief officer Fairfax on his rounds of the ship. Tomorrow Peter would take up his watch-keeping duties and muck in with the rest of the cadets.

Fairfax was a solid, imperturbable man of thirty, a Yorkshireman married to a Northallerton girl who had blessed him with a boy and a girl. He was patient with Peter and explained in detail the workings of this ship whose purpose was so unique.

Marlin was designed to carry a full load of 60,000 tons of oil. Looking forward from the wheelhouse, which was five decks above the main deck, the bows seemed to Peter a long way from the bridge structure — the ship was eight hundred feet long (twelve cricket pitches) with a beam of 110 feet (nearly 40 yards) and a draught of sixty-six feet at extreme load.

As Peter leaned over the stem-head in the bows, he could see the hillock of water being pushed ahead of the bulbous bow which, through a watertight door in the bottom of the ship, could be entered for inspection purposes. The peculiar bow also improved the vessel's handling characteristics at low speeds.

Marlin was modified to transfer oil from only the port side. Two rubber sausages, as large as midget submarines, designed and manufactured in Japan and festooned with gigantic rubber tyres, could be swung over the side from davits spaced one hundred feet apart. Between these fenders, the transfer hoses would swing in their stirrups, slung from the jibs of the cranes. At this position, halfway along the ship's length, the hose connections had to be made, huge alloy flanges that had to be joined by hand and levered tight by muscle power. From here aft, the oil tanks filled the remainder of the hull as far as the citadel. There were seven tanks in all, separated by watertight bulkheads, each tank containing 231,807 cubic feet of fuel.

Peter found it difficult to assimilate the realities of these huge dimensions, but, as the chief officer pointed out, size was relative. Soon there would be half-a-million, then million-ton tankers drawing over one hundred feet and discharging at terminals built on the edge of the Continental Shelf. From these terminals, undersea pipes would transfer the oil to refineries built inland and out of sight of the beauties of the coast.

In addition to the main cargo, were the permanent clean ballast and the slop tanks, both immediately forward of the bridge structure. At the bottom of the ship, in the compartment nearest the tanks, was the pump room which supplied the machinery whereby all this cargo was distributed.

Abaft the pump room was the engine room, in which conventional propelling machinery was installed. Two compact modern boilers, sited at main and poop deck levels, supplied superheated steam to the conventional turbines in the engine room immediately beneath. The turbines, through reduction gearing, drove the single propeller shaft which, revolving through an enormous stern gland, turned the gigantic five-bladed propeller, thirty-six feet in diameter. A balanced rudder, nearly fifty feet in height, was slung less than six feet from the propeller boss. There were no 'A' brackets and the rudder was turned by machinery in the steering gear department immediately above the rudder post.

Control in the engine room was automatic. Temperature readings, lubrication, all the normal chores were carried out through electronic agencies. Direct control of engine movements was exercised through centralized controls in the wheelhouse. At the touch of a button, the Captain could exact immediate response from his engine.

Peter, though astounded by the modern marine technology of this great ship, was even more amazed by the thinking and care that the Pisces Tanker Company had given to the welfare of its officers and crew. Each man felt instinctively that the company which they served had given its utmost to ameliorate the inescapable hardships of life at sea. *Marlin*, a modern ship, was 'General Purpose' manned. Each seaman was trained to work on deck, in the engine room or wherever required by the chief officer or chief engineer. Friction between departments was eliminated and, once the traditional methods of the past were phased out, there could be no doubt as to the advantages of the new system.

Though Peter had been amazed at the standard of living which was assumed to be the norm for this modern tanker, it was the layout of the ship's brain centre, the navigating bridge, which impressed him most.

At the after end was the swimming pool between the two blue funnels, the Pisces logo — a yellow, leaping fish — emblazoned thereon. At night this trademark, recognized the world over for reliability and excellence, was always illuminated by the flood lamps sited at the base of the after screen inside which was the nerve centre of the ship.

On the port side, immediately abaft the bridge, was the combined gyro and radar room, a compartment filled with the most up-to-date equipment. Alongside it, but outside, was the pyrotechnics room, especially protected against fire hazard, where rockets, special flares and signals were stored for immediate use. On the opposite side was the radio room with its small adjunct, the battery room, where the batteries were stored and charged to provide secondary power in emergencies.

The bridge itself was a master's and a navigating officer's dream of perfection. The wheelhouse was entirely enclosed and was combined with the chart room which, an island running athwartships at the after-end of the wheelhouse, was in isolated seclusion yet, through its proximity with the quartermaster and officers of the watch, was in immediate touch with events.

The conventional bridge instruments were sited on the for'd bridge screen, the radar display being to starboard of the wheel. Alongside and in the starboard corner was the radio telephone through which the captain was in touch by voice with any station around the world. It was the radio meteorological report which had just been received that was causing concern in Captain Pelly's mind.

An imminent north-westerly gale warning was broadcast by the BBC, the centre of the depression being over area Shannon. The captain was discussing the latest development with his navigating officer, when finally Peter returned to the bridge after his forenoon's tour of the ship.

'So long as the wind doesn't veer before tomorrow morning,' the master was saying to Hully, where they both bent over the chart table, 'we should benefit by the lee under the Devon cliffs. Better than a southerly gale, though, when we'd have to lighten in the Baie de la Seine.' Captain Pelly smiled as he remembered a particularly unpleasant lightening that he had conducted off Le Havre a few weeks ago. 'I'd much rather be this side, wouldn't you, pilot?'

Hully, addressed by the familiar name adopted by navigating officers, shrugged his shoulders. 'What you gain on the roundabouts, you lose on the swings, sir. There's a better lee here, but the local worthies in the coastal resorts are much fiercer than their French opposite numbers.'

The captain nodded. He had taken immense pains to reassure the inhabitants of Torquay, Paignton and Brixham that the risk of oil pollution during lightening evolutions was virtually nil. Last month a deputation of Aldermen and Mayors had spent the day at sea in *Marlin* while she lightened a V.L.C.C. Not a drop of oil was spilt.

'Tell Sparks to inform *Swordfish* that I'll be in position off Brixham at 1800 and that I expect to begin lightening at 2000.'

A 200,000-ton Pisces V.L.C.C., *Swordfish*, was nearing Ushant after her twenty-nine-day voyage round the Cape. During lightening operations, the 'lightener' was always appointed as senior officer of the operation and was therefore in charge. During this lightening, Captain Pelly was an old friend of *Swordfish*'s master, so the evolution should present no unusual difficulties.

The wind was now freshening and, as Peter sighted the chalk cliffs of The Needles, a tiny white triangle rose crazily on the crest of a breaking wave. Through his binoculars Peter identified a catamaran, outward bound for Cherbourg, She was barely two miles distant and difficult to sight in this flecked sea.

'Every weekend the idiot boys are let loose,' Hully said as he took a bearing of the craft. 'Most of 'em are all right, but the odd fool tries to apply the rule that power gives way to sail. Lord luv-a-duck, but she'll be under our forefoot if she doesn't look out.'

Hully was peering along the azimuth ring of the wing compass repeater. 'Bearing's steady,' he shouted to the captain. 'She's disappearing now, sir.'

'Very good, Mr Hully,' Captain Pelly acknowledged, no hint of irritation in his voice. 'Bring her round forty degrees to starboard.' The helmsman spun his wheel.

'One prolonged blast.'

The navigating officer nodded at Peter who sprinted out to the port bridge screen and yanked at the siren lever. The low sound frequency of the ship's hooter made his ears tingle. He watched the prow of the 80,000-ton tanker slide swiftly across the horizon. She settled on her fresh course, as easy to handle as a frigate.

'From the bridge, we lose sight of a yacht at just under a mile and a half,' Hully said. 'At eighteen knots, she has four minutes in which to take avoiding action. If we don't know she's there, that's not long for an inexperienced yachtsman who may not understand relative change of bearings.'

The catamaran reappeared on the port bow and, as she slid down the port side, the crew were waving.

'They don't realize the speed of approach,' Hully said. 'I dread to think how many boats that disappear are, in fact, run down by ships that don't even know the yacht is there.'

'*Torrey Canyon*,' chipped in Captain Pelly. 'If that disaster can occur through sheer incompetence, anything can.'

The Dorset coast was rearing up above the horizon: Durlston Head, St Albans and Anvil Point. Ahead, a faint smudge grew into the crown of the northern extremity of Portland. At that moment, Sparks came on to the bridge and showed the captain a gale warning report. Captain Pelly strolled to the chart table and picked up the dividers.

'The depression is moving rapidly, pilot,' the master said. 'The wind should veer soon and give us a lee.'

At one-thirty that afternoon, as the Race of Portland frothed and threshed astern of them, the wind obeyed the rules and veered to the north-west as *Marlin* entered Lyme Bay. Though the strength was Force 7, the seas did not get up unreasonably. Brixham, the signal tower on Berry Head and then the Mewstone off the Dartmouth entrance were soon in sight.

Torbay, with its holiday resorts of Torquay and Paignton, began to show above the horizon. Inside the bay, the unfamiliar grey of an aircraft carrier was at anchor.

'*Bulwark*,' Hully said. 'Commando Carrier.' He put down his binoculars. 'There's a Cosmos V.L.C.C., sir,' he reported to his captain. 'At anchor in position D.' Over to starboard, Peter could see the long black hull with its funnel perched up cockily in the stern.

'Brixham Coastguard: good evening, this is *Marlin*.' Captain Pelly was speaking into the hand microphone of the radio telephone. 'Anchoring in position C for Charlie preparatory to lightening procedure with V.L.C.C. *Swordfish*. Can you send out our mails with the pilot, please?'

The domestic arrangements being completed, Captain Pelly talked directly on the R/T with *Swordfish*. She was running into fog off Ushant and did not expect to reach position Charlie before midnight.

'I'll anchor,' the Captain said. 'Check your clearing bearings please, Mr Hully.'

Then, in fourteen fathoms of water and within four miles of Brixham, the starboard anchor was let go.

CHAPTER 13: THE LIGHTENING

Six rapid blasts on the ship's hooter shook Peter from his sleep. In the panic of waking after over-sleeping, he tore out of his bunk; he slipped his uniform over his pyjamas, grabbed his cap and, flailing into his blue sweater, stumbled down the passage for the bridge staircase. As he gained the bridge, the anchor cable was rattling home and from for'd came the clatter of the hands as they rushed in silence to their emergency lightening stations, a routine exercise which was practised before each lightening evolution.

'The six blasts on the hooter are peculiar to *Marlin* and *Tarpon* only,' Hully explained. 'Both lightening captains use this emergency signal so that the drill is standard for both crews.'

Tarpon was *Marlin*'s sister ship, the alternative 'lightener', and used whenever *Marlin* was not available. Both captains commanded either ship as the occasion warranted.

The crew was now closed up at emergency stations. The fire stations were manned, the Martian figures in their asbestos suits crouching over the foam guns sited down the centreline of the main deck. The breakaway party was standing by the port crane, the two chief officers taking charge of the group of men who had gathered together the assortment of breakaway tools required for disconnecting the hoses from the V.L.C.C.: huge spanners, axes, wire strops, scaling ladders and fire extinguishers. All was ready for immediate use in case of an emergency 'breakaway' from the leviathan who would be pumping oil across at one hundred tons a minute. Though it was hazardous and difficult enough to take an 80,000-ton ship alongside a 200,000-ton tanker, it was even more dangerous to break clear if disaster threatened.

The lightening technique, though based on the procedures developed by the whalers in the Antarctic, had been modified by the captains of the Pisces lighteners. After each lightening, more experience had been learnt and 'banked' for future use.

'Secure from emergency lightening stations.'

Captain Pelly put down his microphone, then strolled over to the chart table. 'We'll stooge about off Berry Head until we contact her, pilot,' he said. 'I'll be in my cabin if you need me.'

'Aye, aye, sir.'

It was now dark. Captain Pelly could snatch a respite of three hours provided the fog did not shut down again. Peter spent the first watch on the bridge, keeping a lookout and understudying the officer of the watch. When *Swordfish*'s lights were sighted at 2325, Hully sent him down to report to the captain. During the next hour, the lives of all on board would rest in the hands of that quiet and competent man.

Swordfish was soon in contact on R/T. She reduced speed and turned up under Berry Head to set a course of 120°, as all lightening had to be carried out outside the three-mile limit; Captain Pelly liked at least three miles of sea-room, so the intended track was set at nine miles from the Torbay coast. Peter stood at the back of the port wings of the bridge, navigating officer's notebook in hand to record the captain's orders. He could now see the vast silhouette of *Swordfish*, low in the water and with all her lights extinguished, except for her navigation and warning lights. Behind her were the Torbay illuminations flickering in the background as the gigantic V.L.C.C. slid slowly past.

'Closed up at lightening stations, sir,' Hully reported. '*Swordfish*'s course, one-two-o, speed six knots. Our ship's head, three-one-five; speed six knots.'

'Very good, Mr Hully.'

Peter knew by now that when the captain addressed an officer by 'Mr', that something was in the wind. Captain Pelly stood alone in the port wings, motionless, his face feeling the wind, his eyes becoming accustomed to the darkness. Before lightening, he always wore dark glasses, even in his quarters, so that his sight could be swiftly acclimatized. It took twenty minutes for full night vision to be restored after leaving an illuminated room.

The captain raised the microphone to his lips. 'Control to chief officer. Are you ready to lighten?'

'All ready, sir.' Margesson's voice crackled through the loudspeaker. 'Fenders placed, and breakaway party standing by.'

'Very good; I'm running in now.'

The captain glanced once more at the loom of the V.L.C.C. Peter stood by the door of the wheelhouse to repeat his orders. The officer of the watch was motionless by the engine telegraph handle. The binnacle light glowed an eerie green upon the face of the helmsman. Hully stood facing the doppler log, the reading of which he called out regularly to assist the captain's judgment during the approach. This doppler docking system measured with extreme accuracy the speed of the ship over the ground.

'Range two thousand, one hundred yards, sir,' the officer of the watch reported. '*Swordfish* bearing is drawing ahead.'

'Starboard ten,' the captain ordered. 'Nine-o revolutions.'

'Speed five-and-a-half, sir,' from Hully.

'Hard-a-starboard,' from the captain as he increased the swing.

Marlin's bows were now slipping rapidly across the horizon. Then, as they caught up on *Swordfish*'s quarter, Captain Pelly was certain that he was safely within the turning circle.

'Ease to ten.'

'Ease to ten, sir,' from the quartermaster as he spun his stainless steel wheel.

'Steer one-two-five.'

'Steer one-two-five, sir.' Then, a quarter of a minute later, 'Course, sir: one-two-five.'

So much depended on the helmsman who, when lightening, was always the senior quartermaster. A mistake the wrong way on the wheel; the inevitable collision and the ensuing holocaust: much depended on the skill and concentration of that man of twenty-three on the wheel.

The captain had picked up his R/T microphone. 'What's your course and speed, please, captain?' he enquired of *Swordfish*'s master. 'I'm running in now. Over.'

The loudspeaker instantly crackled in reply.

'This is *Swordfish*. One-one-nine, four knots. Nice to see you again, Captain Pelly.' The dialogue was unconcerned, friendly and entirely confident. 'It's all yours now. Over.'

'Thank you very much. My speed five-and-a-half. Please steady on one-one-nine.'

The only sound now came from *Marlin*'s fo'c'sle where the clatter of the wires being hauled out broke the stillness. Peter could distinguish the figures of men standing motionless on *Swordfish*'s starboard side. They seemed like puppets on that gigantic upper deck, marionettes that moved with little urgency. The mental lethargy of the V.L.C.C. crews after their twenty-nine days of monotonous voyaging from Bahrein and around The Cape, was a notorious hazard known as 'Cape Disease'. After such a long spell, the sailor's reaction to any emergency was sluggish and, sometimes, nil. *Marlin* had once hurled lines across for a quick hauling in of the berthing wires. The monkey's fists of the heaving lines had clattered at the feet of the V.L.C.C.'s crew who, listlessly chatting across the water gap, responded slowly to the urgency. This 'disease' was now recognized and the crew from the lighteners were ready to scramble across on the ladder to assist.

'Range, sir, four hundred yards,' Hully reported. 'Speed five knots.'

'Very good, pilot. Steer one-one-o.'

Marlin had been running in at right angles on *Swordfish*'s starboard side. As the vast bulk of the V.L.C.C. loomed up ahead, *Marlin* had rounded up and, though steaming up alongside, was closing the distance by steering a slightly converging course.

'Three-forty yards, sir. Speed, five knots.'

The seconds passed. Only the captain's orders could be heard above the background of the wind.

'Steer one-one-five. Six-o revolutions.'

The blare of the telegraph repeater made Peter jump. He could see now *Swordfish*'s captain, a small figure in the starboard wings of the V.L.C.C. He was raising a microphone to his lips as he leaned over to judge the distance:

'My course one-one-nine. My speed four decimal one.'

'Roger.' Captain Pelly had now moved out to the port wing. From there he could assess better the distance of the gap and the relative differences in speed.

'Stop engine,' he rapped. 'Lights on.'

The whole of *Swordfish*'s side suddenly gleamed, her plates rust-streaked from the long voyage. *Marlin*'s scuppers towered above the V.L.C.C.'s main deck some twenty feet below, a deck that shielded the huge bulk of oil beneath. *Marlin*'s fo'c'sle head was as light as day and the lamps at the jib heads of the cranes flooded the area abaft the breakwater.

'Fifty yards, sir.'

'Very good, Mr Hully. Six-o revolutions.'

Peter peered over the side. The gap between the two tankers was lessening at every second. The seas chopped between the ships, hissing and breaking in confusion.

'Steer one-one-seven.'

Marlin was coming alongside thirty yards too far ahead. The for'd fenders were about to take the crunch.

'Hard-a-starboard. Five-o revolutions.'

Abreast the bridge, thirty feet clear. There was no sound on the bridge, no movement. The captain had his eyes glued on *Marlin*'s bows which suddenly began to swing to starboard.

'Lost steerage way,' the helmsman shouted, a note of anxiety in his voice.

'Midships.'

The ship shuddered as the for'd fender squelched. The stern swung in. The two hulls were bearing forward and aft. The captain leaned over the port bridge wing. Speed was now the vital ingredient for a successful transfer. The headrope was already across and the springs were going out.

'Stop engine. Hard-a-port.'

As *Swordfish* continued ahead on her majestic way, *Marlin* gently slipped astern until the weight came on the back spring. Finally she was secured, her crane abreast *Swordfish*'s manifold. Both ships stopped engines and took off their way. *Swordfish*'s anchor cable rattled, her bell chimed. *Marlin* waited for *Swordfish* to swing to the wind and tide before the decision was taken to make the hose connections.

All hands on deck were now in overalls and all wore safety helmets. The back spring was surged on *Swordfish*'s winch until *Marlin*'s crane jib steadied abreast *Swordfish*'s manifold. The alloy portable gangway was slung across; then John Fairfax scrambled across on all fours, a rope around his shoulders and followed by two seamen carrying a large wheel-spanner and tommy-bar, to help make the connections at *Swordfish*'s end.

The crane motors whined as the jibs elevated to plumb the stirrups which carried the transfer hose. Heaving lines fluttered across and the hose was hauled over by *Swordfish*. The cranes were then carefully adjusted until the right-angled bend in the hose was opposite *Swordfish*'s manifold. Fairfax, pushing aside the onlookers on board *Swordfish*, wrestled with the huge brass flange until finally it snapped on to *Swordfish*'s pipe. A quick wrench with the giant wheel-spanner and the connection was made.

Philip Margesson, who was carefully watching events from *Marlin*, raised his walkie-talkie microphone.

'Control: hose-connections made, sir. Ready to take in cargo.'

'Start pumping.' There was the same imperturbability in Captain Pelly's voice as had been exercised during the whole of this hazardous night.

Peter had been sent down to the crane to see how the evolution was progressing. The hose was now pulsating as the oil flowed across in the gigantic transfer pipe. Chief officer Margesson was just checking the input flow when a cry floated across the space between the ships, Peter looked up and there was a man looking up from *Swordfish*'s rail, his face contorted with fear.

'Back spring's parted,' he yelled.

Margesson tore at his walkie-talkie:

'Back spring's parted, sir.'

A second's silence.

'Very good, Mr Margesson. Breakaway.' The captain's voice crackling through the walkie-talkie was calm, decisive.

Then, as Philip Margesson shouted to the men already running back towards the crane, *Marlin* began to move. Slowly at first, inch by inch, then faster until the black hull was sliding down *Swordfish*'s side.

'*Breakaway!*' Margesson yelled at the gaping man standing by *Swordfish*'s complex of valves. '*Shut down. Disconnect the hose...*'

His voice was drowned by the blasts for Emergency Lightening Stations. As men rushed to their Fire Stations, the gangway between the ships tilted crazily. Fairfax, who was halfway across, scrambled back on board *Swordfish*, leaping across her guard rails as the gangway crashed down between the ships.

'All gone for'd,' a voice shouted from the fo'c'sle head. Then as the breakaway party began hacking at the hose with axes, the jib of the crane crumpled. There was a noise of rasping metal and suddenly a vivid flash.

Peter felt the searing flame. He saw a man fall, smelt the acrid smell of burning fumes. There was a shout from Margesson and suddenly a rushing noise that engulfed them all. Peter choked as the foam from the midship fire cannon smothered the area where they stood in stupefied bewilderment.

'God! Look at that.'

Peter followed the direction of the man's outstretched hand. Dancing across the gauze protecting the exhaust vent of number five tank was a small blue flame.

Peter knew again the meaning of terror. Here they were, powerless to save themselves, standing on top of an empty tank full of fumes. If that flame penetrated the gauze, they'd all be blown to kingdom come. Hypnotized by the flame dancing in the vent, Peter was bowled over by the force of the foam as it struck. The whole of his world went white. He choked as he fell.

Slithering on all fours across the slippery deck, Peter felt a hand grasping him by the collar. Then he was hauled clear, gasping for breath.

'Give us a hand,' chief petty officer Hawkins shouted. 'The fore spring.'

They scrambled for'd as fast as the foam would allow.

Marlin's bows had now paid off. She was falling away rapidly to leeward. The fore spring was slack in the water but, as Peter and Hawkins reached the port bollard, the bight began to take up.

'Quick, for Pete's sake!' Hawkins yelled. 'Stand clear if we can't slip it.'

They hurled themselves at the eye of the wire and, as the bight threshed clear of the water, they wrestled with the eye to slip it over the lip of the bollard. The wire snaked out through the fairlead and disappeared with a splash into the sea which boiled between the ships who were now fifty feet apart.

'Near one,' said the chief petty officer. 'Once saw a guy pulled through a bull-ring. Wasn't much left of him.' He shook his head and hurried towards the manifold.

Incredibly, no one had been seriously hurt. Miraculously, there had been no fire, no calamitous explosion. By the time the shambles on deck had been sorted out, the wind had moderated. Captain Pelly decided to continue with the lightening and, three-quarters of an hour later, had again taken *Marlin* alongside *Swordfish*. The ships were secured once more, the springs being doubled up. The spare transfer hose was sent across, this time slung entirely from *Swordfish*'s crane. A problem arose when the connection had to be made.

Swordfish's main flange had been badly distorted at the breakaway, so the normal connection on the manifold could not be used. She fortunately possessed a stand-by pipeline which she often used in the American refineries. By using a special adaptor piece at both ends, the oil could be pumped across through the hose.

This time there were no accident. The hose was hauled into place and the American adaptor, a cunning box of tricks that needed considerable manipulation and skill to assemble, finally made the connection after everyone at the manifold, including Peter, had tried his hand at fitting the special flange.

Pumping began and soon the night settled into normal routine as the oil gushed into the lightening tanker.

The December dawn was bitterly cold. Peter, who had the morning watch, stood for a moment on the starboard bridge wing, blowing on his mittened fingers as he listened to a ship's siren in the distance to the southward. Thick fog now swirled around the anchored tankers. Apart from the gurgling of the tide running between the ships, the only sound was the occasional mewing of a tern and the foghorns of distant ships.

The scene had changed radically. *Marlin*, now three-quarters full of oil, was settling deeper into the water and showing only ten feet of freeboard. *Swordfish*, emptied of some fifty thousand tons of fuel, was towering above her diminutive consort, the V.L.C.C.'s upper deck now being twenty feet higher than *Marlin*'s. Two more hours and the lightening would be complete.

Peter re-entered the wheelhouse. He would write up the log, then make coffee for the officer of the watch and the quartermaster. As he collected together his weather readings his mind began to wander. Visibility was shutting down for'd.

This tanker life was unique. With the risks that the crew accepted as part of their daily lives, the officers and men had every reason to feel inwardly that they belonged to an elite corps of seafarers. They were proud men, jealous of their professional competence, but devoid of arrogance. Like men of achievement the world over, the more they had experienced and suffered, the more they learned of humility. The attitude of the nation, which seemed to take the merchant service for granted, certainly emphasized the quality of reticence.

Only six weeks ago a Pisces V.L.C.C. (*Bonito*, wasn't she?) had suffered an explosion in number four centre tank. Madagascar had passed astern when there was a flash and a violent explosion. The plates of the main deck above the tank had been ripped upwards. One seaman, who had been standing by a valve, was blown to smithereens. The fourth engineer, who had been servicing the engine of the starboard lifeboat, was blown over the side. He, too, was never seen again, in spite of a five-hour search by *Bonito* after the accident.

The flame from the explosion had enveloped the bridge. Curling back abaft the structure, the heat had caused terrible injuries to the few women who were sunbathing by the swimming pool. The cause of the accident was unknown but believed to be connected with the washing valves which, in *Bonito*, were of a fixed variety, unlike those in *Marlin* which were flexible and lowered by hand into the tank. Static electricity was believed to have been induced and, for some unexplained reason, suddenly earthed. The resulting spark was believed to have been the cause of the disaster.

It was danger that forged the comradeship amongst the tankermen. Like submariners, each man depended upon his messmate. One man's carelessness could kill them all.

Peter gazed for'd into the fog. Nothing there — a pale glare, a ghostly fo'c'sle with her bows invisible in the swirling mist. His eyes ached with searching, but the radar P.P.I. was not always reliable. The watch was dragging but breakfast could not be far off now for the hands were coming up from below and mustering on the main deck. They looked a splendid bunch and Peter hoped he would be in *Marlin* long enough really to know them. Every member of the crew was an established man, contracted by the company to serve for a specified period. This bond bred loyalty on both sides.

The chief petty officer was detailing the hands. Margesson was inspecting the crumpled jib of the crane. The seamen dispersed to their various jobs: stowing gear, collecting tommy-bars, mustering spare gaskets, axes and heaving lines.

Then, swiftly, the fog lifted to disclose the bows. The captain came on the bridge. Pumping stopped, the hose was disconnected. By eight-thirty the anchor had clanked home. The company flag was hoisted and, midst farewells between both ships, *Marlin* broke away.

Fredericia in Northern Denmark was the next port of call in which to discharge cargo — eight hundred miles away and through the Dover Straits. Fog was forecast and fifteen hundred ships a day passed through that Dover bottleneck. Captain Pelly was uncommunicative as he set course up-channel.

CHAPTER 14: THE STRAITS

The fog lasted for three and a half hours. The forenoon watch seemed interminable, as the laden tanker proceeded at five knots up the English Channel. From the bridge, her bows vanished once more into the swirling vapours. The huge fenders were swung inboard; a lookout was posted in the eyes of the ship. Once every two minutes a prolonged, five-second blast reverberated through the stillness of the morning, echoing into the fog.

The captain never left the bridge. His eyes were riveted to the fluorescent light of the radar scan, his concentration balancing the relative changes of bearing of the different echoes. So long as all other shipping obeyed the International Regulations for Preventing Collisions at Sea, there was no excessive hazard provided that the radar operated efficiently — and in *Marlin* there was the standby if the main set broke down. It was the rogue ship, the irresponsible fool who constituted the nightmare threat. The ship that deliberately flouted the recommended shipping laws and came pounding down against the stream was the lunatic menace. With ships carrying 200,000 tons of crude oil now using the Channel, the risk of appalling disaster was always present.

'Look at that oil slick, Mr Sinclair,' Captain Pelly said, interrupting the musings of his young deck cadet. 'One of the worst I've seen. There's a ship ahead of us and that filth is the discharge from her tank cleaning.'

'Can't we stop them, sir?' Peter asked as he gazed down on the filthy sea, streaked for miles by the effluent from a tanker's dirty bunkers. Birds were hovering above the man-made filth, fear already ingrained into their instincts: to alight in that oily element meant death to them.

'How can you — in fog?' the master replied. 'If a ship's captain can be irresponsibly wicked like this, there's only one way to solve the problem and that is by the certainty of detection.'

'Almost impossible, sir?'

'I'd have a United Nations Inspection Service. Any ship coming up-Channel would be boarded off Ushant by an official — an extension of the pilot service, if you like. He would remain on board until the ship reached her port of discharge. This inspection service would be backed up by helicopter and coastguard vessels, manned and paid for by the United Nations or by the countries whose shores butted on the shipping lanes.'

Peter's mind was grappling with the menace. When he was Captain Pelly's age, the problem would either have been cured or the planet would be breathing its last. 'One day the world will wake up, I suppose, sir,' he said quietly. 'Unless we police the whole surface, there'll be no people to whom the ships need ply their trade.'

'The problem is as serious as that,' the captain said. 'Maybe our politicians will learn to deal with the vital issues, instead of pecking amongst themselves. At least they've made a start with the U.N.O. Environment Conference in Sweden.'

The Captain returned to the wheelhouse to check the radar scan. Peter watched the deck party working on the tanks, measuring, checking, securing the wires. One of the big Japanese fender wires had taken a turn round the drum and this was causing trouble to clear. The regulations for the safe-working-loads of all wires, winches and machinery in this ship were rigidly enforced and the routine tests were never overlooked by the chief officers who relied much upon their chief petty officer, Bill Hawkins. Peter could not help but admire this man who, only twenty-six years old, led so admirably the men under his charge. Hawkins was always leading from the front; a keen dinghy sailor (he stowed his boat in the forepeak), he was a competent and knowledgeable seaman. He regularly attended the Supervisors' Courses run at Westcliff-on-Sea by the British Shipping Federation for petty officers and leading rates. There he met others whose genuine interest was the merchant service; through their discussions they kept abreast of modern development and, by their influence, improved the efficiency of working their ships.

Visibility cleared at 1100, when Portland Bill was sighted ten miles off *Marlin*'s bow. As the fog banks unrolled, yellow and dirty green, the shapes of shipping on parallel courses emerged through the murk as they plodded up-Channel. *Marlin* increased speed to eighteen knots but it was sunset before Beachy Head came abeam. Captain Pelly, keeping south of the twenty fathom line, left the *Royal Sovereign* light vessel to port, then rounded up to set course to the eastward of the Varne Bank.

The disappearance of the watery sun introduced the cold conditions for a reappearance of surface fog. With visibility reduced to three miles, the captain eased the ship's speed to ten knots until the flashing lights of the Varne light vessel came in sight. Three sunken ships lay there, victims of their own incompetence. The wreck buoys winked their green warnings; the lightship was continually alert to warn off approaching ships, yet the occasional lunatic still blundered onwards.

By 2300 *Marlin* had passed through the narrow Straits of Dover. The *Dyck* lightship flashed on her starboard bow, then the Sandettie Bank light, to port.

'They're beginning to bunch,' the master said to Hully who had been permanently on the bridge for the past eight hours. 'How far off is the Cosmos V.L.C.C. now?'

'Just over a mile, sir. Bearing is steady.'

'I'll reduce speed if we haven't left her astern by the time we reach the West Hinder. Reckon she's Euro bound.'

The Cosmos V.L.C.C. had remained on that bearing ever since the Isle of Wight. A gap of a mile was not much in these restricted waters. There was a large general cargo ship ahead and, on their port quarter, a modern container ship with her upper deck lights blazing, cracking up astern and trying to overtake.

Visibility shut down to a mile and a half. The V.L.C.C.'s lights became a blur, her port light a faint glow. She seemed very close.

'Don't like it,' the captain said. 'Slow ahead.'

The telegraph repeat buzzed.

'Start the hooter, Mr Sinclair.'

Peter stayed by the lever on the port screen. He peered ahead, his eyes aching. As the hand of his wristwatch came up at each minute, he blasted the hooter until his head ached from the reverberations. The V.L.C.C., unable to alter to starboard because of the depth of water, was almost leaning on their starboard bow; the container ship was breathing down their necks. It was at that moment that Peter saw the faint smudge dead ahead. He looked again, unable to believe his eyes.

'Fishing boat, starboard bow, sir,' he shouted.

Captain Pelly had also sighted the boat, a trawling smack from out of Dunkirk or Gravelines. Her port light was so faint that it was invisible until a ship was on top of her.

'Lunatic!' the captain swore quietly to himself, the first time that Peter had heard him explode. 'Full astern. Hard-a-starboard.'

Hully nodded at Peter. 'Three blasts,' he shouted, 'followed by one.'

The helmsman had spun his wheel and already *Marlin*'s bows were beginning to swing.

The ship's hooter boomed into the night. The trawler, now with three white lights blazing from its foremast, disappeared under *Marlin*'s bows, her mizzen sail a black triangular patch. Then Peter saw the V.L.C.C.

Her port quarter was now at less than a cable, her huge funnel and bridge upperworks like mediaeval battlements looming in the night.

'Emergency Stations,' Captain Pelly snapped. Hully jumped to the alarm push. He stabbed at it five times.

Peter, standing by the hooter lever, watched with horror the approaching disaster.

'Let go the starboard anchor.' It was the Captain's voice, passing his order down the fo'c'sle phone.

Then the sound rattled up towards the bridge: the cacophony of the cable running unchecked through the hawsepipe, a twenty-ton anchor plummeting to the seabed. The ship was now shuddering from the full astern power of the massive propeller. The log was indicating three knots and its pointer was falling to its stop as she lost way.

'Lost steerage way, sir.' There was fear in the helmsman's cry. The cable was now clanking intermittently and between the spasms Peter could hear the shouts of the men on the main deck rushing to their fire stations. He watched as the fire gun crew at number three station tore at the nozzle-securing clamp, their faces turned upwards towards the monster that was about to crush them. Peter barely noticed the French fishing boat careering down the port side, the crew shaking their fists and singing the *Marseillaise*, in grotesque discord.

Marlin was now trembling along the whole length of her hull. She had lost all way and was fast gathering sternway.

'Off brake and clear the fo'c'sle head.'

There was now nothing further that anybody could do: nothing but pray. The captain stood motionless at the bridge windows, facing towards the black hull now sliding swiftly up the starboard side. Its superstructure was as huge as a Highland castle but, to Peter's amazement, the V.L.C.C.'s wake threshed white, her propeller churning ahead at full speed. The rudder head was tipping the swirling waters and was hard-over to port. Her captain had sized up the situation when he had heard the rattle of *Marlin*'s anchor. Unable to swing to starboard because he was on the southern limit of the Channel, he had realized there was only one chance remaining to him: to try and pass ahead, swinging his stern away as he did so.

The plating of the V.L.C.C.'s transom slid into view, squarely towards them, *Tolco Amsterdam* of Glasgow. Her port lifeboat was now hanging above the fo'c'sle head, her port quarter abreast the circle of the helicopter pad.

'She's swinging to port,' Captain Pelly said quietly. 'Wheel hard-a-starboard, Quartermaster.' *Marlin* responded immediately. Her bows swung to port, slowly, then turned swiftly. They waited on the bridge, holding their breaths for the shriek of mangled metal, the sparks, the fireball of the explosion and — oblivion. The V.L.C.C.'s port quarter slid up the starboard bow, under the flare and — passed ahead.

No one knew by how much they missed. No one cared. The gigantic transom crossed their bows and swiftly diminished, forgotten now that the collision was averted.

'Stop engine,' the Captain ordered. 'Emergency Full Ahead.' The telegraph rang twice and was as rapidly answered, A brief lull and then *Marlin* trembled from the sudden power.

'Near one,' Captain Pelly murmured. 'Thought I'd lost my anchor.'

Peter gulped: this was the understatement of the year. If the two captains had not been of the highest calibre, superbly trained and served by first-class officers and men, a terrible disaster would have occurred. He wondered how long it would be before the inevitable took place. The sooner the Dover Straits were internationally controlled with statutory shipping routes, the less chance of disaster.

The V.L.C.C. plodded onwards, altering course to starboard off the mouth of the Scheldt. Her master had signalled laconically on the R/T: 'Never knew you cared,' to which Captain Pelly replied, 'Absence makes the heart grow fonder.' That was all. In the privacy of his cabin he had expressed himself more forcefully when Peter had reported to him with a Marconigram.

'All part of the seafarer's routine, Mr Sinclair. While fishing boats drawing six feet still have right of way over tankers drawing sixty feet in restricted waters, near-disasters like that will occur every night. They do it deliberately, you know.'

The captain slit open the signal, perused it carefully, then without a word handed it to his deck cadet.

'*Marlin* from Pisces,' Peter read. 'Cadet Sinclair is to be discharged on arrival at Fredericia. He is to report forthwith to Liverpool agent who will arrange attendance at Magistrates' Court. Confidential details for Master to follow.'

Peter, feeling the colour draining from his face, read the message twice to regain his composure. He looked up to find Captain Pelly's eyes boring steadily into him.

'I had hoped to have you longer.' The remark was a reproach. Peter wished that the carpet on which he stood would swallow him up. 'You're a fool to become implicated in this sort of thing, Mr Sinclair. You may tell me about it if you wish.'

The interview lasted half an hour. It was not until Peter had closed the door of the captain's cabin behind him that he appreciated how much the captain had helped. After a long day and night on the bridge, when he must have been mentally and physically exhausted, Captain Pelly had still drawn upon his reserves to try and help his young and foolish cadet. Such men were the backbone of the merchant service. They still gave of themselves and still did not count the cost, whatever attitudes the rest of society adopted.

'If you are cleared by the court,' he had concluded, 'you are welcome back in my ship. You've done well, and I'll give you a good report.'

Eighteen hours later, *Marlin* went alongside the oiling jetty at the refinery in Fredericia, the clean and miniscule port inside the neck of Denmark.

Rounding the Skaw during the mists of an early morning, the northern lights flickering in their splendour above the horizon, *Marlin* reduced speed to pick up the Danish pilot from the orange-coloured boat that chugged alongside.

'Good luck, Sinclair,' Fairfax said later when Peter hesitated by the gangway. 'We'll make a tanker-man of you yet.' He had grasped Peter's hand and slapped him on the back, a gesture that had heartened Peter as he strode towards the railway station that was the beginning of his journey to Esbjerg and the North Sea ferry to Harwich. Whatever lay ahead, he knew now how splendid life in the Merchant Navy could be. He'd return to tankers, however painful his experiences with the court and his involvement with Penny might prove to be.

CHAPTER 15: ALTERATION OF COURSE

They had taken a bus out to Hoylake after the Magistrate's judgment. Peter had been shocked by the finding and the result of the £100 fine imposed on Penny. She had maintained her composure in the court but, sitting in silence upstairs in the front of the double-decker, he felt her body convulsed by the sobs that she had tried to stifle. They had walked the dunes, the cold of that January day cutting into their skins so that their cheeks were burning when finally they found shelter by the fireside of the local inn. They had sat in silence, staring into the flickering flames, alone in the low-beamed room. She had taken his hand and laid her head upon his shoulder for comfort. He had stroked her hair then, content to share her troubles. 'It's the unfairness of it all,' she whispered. 'To think that Morgan escaped scot-free.'

'The police will be after him,' Peter said. 'He'll be a hunted man.'

It was the injustice, even more than Finnimore's rejection of Penny, that rankled. According to the police, Interpol had traced the source of information to Bombay where a seaman called Gokal Bhoj, the ex-deck tindal of *Exmouth Haven*, had informed against Finnimore in particular, and the rest of the junior officers in general. Bhoj was apparently nursing some grievance against the officers, the police inspector had reported, but undoubtedly Finnimore, who had vanished into thin air, was the main culprit.

So Peter was discharged, after a sobering remonstrance from the magistrate. Penny was allowed twelve months in which to pay her fine because of her further nursing training, but, if after that time she had not paid up, she would be sent to prison for three months. An example had to be made of her complicity, the magistrate pronounced, to deter other foolish young ladies: he would have sentenced her more severely had her background been different.

Peter had been immensely impressed by the majesty of the law and, in particular, by the manner in which the court leaned over backwards to be fair to the defendants. Then, Penny having been found guilty, how justice had been tempered with mercy to give her every possible chance.

'At least you'll be able to start your nursing,' Peter said, tightening his arm about her. 'The judgment hasn't affected your career provided you pay the fine.'

'The solicitor said there was no point in appealing,' she said. 'But how am I going to raise the money? I can only just exist as it is.'

A wave of compassion swept through Peter. He was fond of Penny, this mysterious girl alone in the world.

'Penny,' he said impulsively. 'Let me help. Why don't you start your course at the hospital as planned, and forget the money. I'll raise it for you. You can pay me back later.'

She had protested at first, putting forward every objection, when finally she was persuaded. A wave of happiness had swept over him as she had cried with relief into his shoulder. Later, he put her on the train at Lime Street; he watched her hand disappearing from view as she waved through the window of the carriage which twisted away round the bend of the track.

As he retraced his steps down the platform, he quickened his pace towards the row of public telephone boxes. He flipped open the pages of the directory. His finger slid down the columns of Gs: there it was, Globe Tanker Company in bold, black letters — down by the Liver Building. He slipped the book back into its nook, shoved open the door, and began hurrying towards the city centre.

The assistant marine superintendent in the Globe Tankers' office had been brisk but helpful. Yes, it was true that the Company employed Acting Fourth Officers: Deck Cadets who, having passed their Second Mates' Board of Trade Exams, were doing their final Sea Phase for the three-year time qualification, or while waiting for their twentieth birthday. Yes, Globe Tankers did pay high salaries to their officers, but this policy was in compensation for the conditions under which their officers operated: for instance, the ships were basically fast barges which could transport the maximum amount of crude oil to refineries all over the world in the shortest possible time at the highest profit margin. The sharp-featured official had concluded by suggesting that Peter reapplied for an appointment as soon as he was qualified — after he had finished his Phase III Shore Training at the Warsash Navigation School.

Peter's mind was made up. He had given his word to Penny and somehow he would save enough money to pay her fine within the year. He could at least join Globe Tankers and quickly save the cash, whereas Penny had no chance on a nurse's salary. When he left Liverpool, he had no time to visit his father as he was due at the Plymouth College of Technology by 1600 on the following day.

Four-and-a-half months in the department of marine studies would see him through his Phase I and then he would apply again to Captain Pelly for reappointment to *Marlin*. There could be no better ship in which to serve his minimum nine months sea service for Phase II.

The spell in college flew by, a period in which Peter had to work his utmost in order to keep up with the O.N.C. syllabus. His Record Book from sea had been carefully scrutinized when he had joined the college, the principal apparently being satisfied that Peter had thoroughly prepared for the subjects to be studied.

Though Peter had enjoyed his four-and-a-half months in Plymouth, Phase I of the course was marred for him by the growing realization that he was going to find it impossible to save the £100 for Penny's fine. The worry developed into a repressed anxiety so that, by the time he left Plymouth, he longed to share his troubles with someone he could trust. It was not surprising therefore that, during the two days he spent at home with his father, his dilemma spilled into a spate of words to which the older man listened in silence.

Peter's father, apart from expressing forcibly his opinion of Peter's gullibility, did not condemn. Instead, when asked for advice, he agreed that Peter, when he had sat for his second mate's ticket, should join the notorious Globe Tanker Fleet in order to raise the money quickly,

'It'll be too late, I'm afraid,' Peter had murmured. 'Penny has only another seven months in which to pay.'

The father had changed the subject then and for the rest of the forty-eight hours' leave, the delicate subject had not been mentioned again.

To Peter's delight, his request to rejoin *Marlin* was approved by Captain Pelly, now that Peter had been cleared of the police charge. Peter boarded the lightening tanker once again, but this time at the Tranmere Refinery, near Liverpool. He was welcomed back and very soon was made to feel once again part of the team in that fine ship. She turned round in twenty-four hours so it was to be ten days, after another visit to Fredericia, before Peter opened the mail that awaited them on their return to Thames Haven.

He opened the letter that was addressed to him in his father's neat handwriting. The note inside was typical:

'Pete,' his father wrote. 'You are a fool to have promised the young lady money which you did not have. I want you to do well during your next year in Phase II, your sea service in *Marlin*. If you worry yourself with meeting a promise you cannot keep, you will fail in your career and I want you to give of your best to Captain Pelly. You have given your word to this girl. You have learned your lesson, so please accept the enclosed, with my affection.

'Please pay back the loan as soon as you can because, with this sickening inflation, a retired man's resources are shrinking every day. Yours aye, Dad.'

Folded in a scrap of paper was a pink cheque made out to him for the sum of one hundred pounds.

Peter stood motionless, staring through the scuttle of his small cabin. His eyes were moist, and he felt the emotion choking him as he fought back the wave of affection which engulfed him. He'd write to Penny, asking for the address to which he should send the money for the payment of the fine. He wished that he could personally hand the money to her: but life in *Marlin* for a junior officer was so hectic that he had no time in which to visit his young nurse.

Penny wrote back to thank him, but her letter had been short: she was very busy and, Peter guessed, probably embarrassed now by the whole affair. Peter had shrugged his shoulders and thrown himself into the business of living. All he wanted now was to do well in *Marlin* so that his Record Book and Master's Report would be adequate for the last stage of his training, Phase III at the Warsash Navigation School.

Peter was nineteen years and eight months old when eventually, after a crowded and happy year into which was squeezed a tanker safety course, he left *Marlin* for his final shore-training at the mouth of the Hamble River, that overcrowded yachting centre at the entrance to Southampton Water. He had become part of *Marlin* and hated leaving her; but it was a pleasant change to enjoy the spell ashore which culminated in the Board of Trade Examination for the Second Mate's Certificate of Competency and the Ordinary National Certificate in Nautical Science.

He spent six months at Warsash, twenty-four weeks of intensive study in the practical requirements of navigation, seamanship, and cargo-stowage. A radar course was included and when eventually the date arrived for the examination, Peter's head was crammed to capacity. He made good friends at Warsash, a unique nautical training establishment which prided itself on its discipline and thorough training.

The termly fees, as at Plymouth, were paid by the Shipping Companies, and were augmented by 'grants in aid' for the Phase III courses. Yet, even so, Peter found that he had to be very careful with the little money he had saved to see him through. Then at last came the ordeal of the examination: a week of strain which alternated hope and despair.

The results came through when Peter had flopped home to recuperate. He had passed, albeit somewhere near the bottom of the list, but he had passed and now possessed his second mate's ticket. Now to sea, as an acting fourth officer: he could not join *Atlas*, Globe's crack tanker quickly enough. The company would fly him to Pernambuco, the agent said, if he could be ready in time.

CHAPTER 16: THE BULK CARRIER

The V.L.C.C. *Atlas*, of the Globe Tanker Company, was due in Bahia, on the eastern coast of Brazil, in thirty-six hours' time. Peter had barely time to collect his tropical uniform of white shirts, shorts and long whites, before the Boeing 707 took off from Heathrow for Lisbon. During the flight across the Atlantic, from Lisbon to Recife, he had time in which to reflect on his progress so far in his seafaring career. Though he was no genius, he had at least passed his Board of Trade Examinations for Second Mate, which vital certificate he would be granted when he had qualified for his sea-service time: another twelve months at sea for him, making a total of three years.

Captain Pelly and Pisces had been very understanding by allowing him to be seconded to Globe, an American subsidiary of Pisces. Because of this loose affiliation between the two companies, a three-year deck cadet was allowed promotion to uncertificated officer during the last six months of his sea service. Though this sea-time was counted as qualifying service, the regulations stated that the whole of the deck cadet's qualifying sea service after promotion to uncertificated officer would incur a penalty by increasing this time by a third. For Peter, this was a small price to pay for the opportunity to repay his debt to his father. He would have to serve in *Atlas* for twelve months instead of nine. He would then be twenty years and eleven months, eleven months older than the minimum age qualification of twenty for a Qualified Officer.

He smiled to himself as the coastline of Brazil filtered through the blue haze thousands of feet below them. There was Recife, stretching along the white-fringed seaboard; he would have to wait there for two hours in the heat before catching the DC-9 for Salvador.

Atlas was already berthed on the bunkering jetty when Peter rattled alongside in the old Cadillac taxi. He stood squinting upwards into the glaring sunlight at the vessel towering above him. Totally different from the fine lines of *Marlin*, the American V.L.C.C. was a giant oil barge, devoid of any redeeming aesthetic attraction. With her light-grey plating almost red-hot in the equatorial sun; with her square transom, her huge bulbous bow and slab sides without a suspicion of a sheer, *Atlas* resembled an enormous caricature of a hippopotamus at its waterhole, stationary, comatose in the sun: ugly, but functional. The battery of fuelling hoses pulsated in the windless air but no one was to be seen in this torrid heat. Peter felt a reluctance to join this ship which, for taxation purposes, flew the Liberian flag of convenience, a red, white and blue affair which, without pride, hung limply from her stern. He squared his shoulders, picked up his two grips and, the sweat pouring down his back, clambered up the long gangway.

There was no one at the brow but two men were working on the readings, slouched in the pool of shade cast from the port lifeboat on the deck above. The larger of the two was an officer in a soiled khaki shirt, shorts and sandals. He was tall, even as he stooped, and Peter waited a moment before making himself known. He put down his bags, and the clatter diverted the concentration of the two men. The seaman, a dark-skinned Brazilian, turned and, smiling briefly, continued with the readings. Then the officer faced him. Peter caught his breath as his eyes swept to the name tally on the officer's shirt. 'M. G. Philmore,' he read, 'Fourth Officer — UK.' The eyes of the two men met before Philmore looked away. The man's face was familiar: flaxen, over-long hair, pushing out beneath his cap; the pale blue eyes, too close together, that exuded a craftiness impossible to conceal. The heavy shoulders which bore too much flesh had begun to stoop.

'You're Mr Sinclair, aren't you? We're expecting you.' He tucked the register board beneath his arm and turned to the boat deck ladder. 'Follow me. I'll take you to the mate.'

Peter picked up his bags and hurried after the fair-haired officer who had now stopped in the shade by the port lifeboat where no one could overhear their conversation. Peter dumped his bags but declined the hand that was outstretched towards him. He knew now that he had not been mistaken.

'I shouldn't adopt that attitude, Sinclair,' sneered Morgan Finnimore. 'It doesn't become a druggie.' There was a glint in his eyes; hate or fear, Peter could not be sure.

'How d'you get here?' Peter asked quietly. 'They've been searching for you for five months now.'

'Mind your own business,' Finnimore snapped, 'and don't ask questions. This ship's like the Foreign Legion: we're all here with something to hide.' He laughed shortly. 'And you're no different, are you?' He put his face close to Peter's. 'You've never seen me before, right? I worked fast to get here. Slipped out before the net closed. I'm safe here, so don't you breathe a word or…' He grabbed Peter's wrist and dug his fingers deep into the flesh, a sudden movement with immense strength. 'I'll kill you, Sinclair, if you split.' The words were whispered, and then he tapped the tally on his chest. 'That's my name, and don't you forget it.'

He swung away. The scene was spent. He walked to the screen door and raised his voice:

'This way, Mr Sinclair. The chief officer's expecting you.'

Three months elapsed before Peter realized what Finnimore was up to — three long months with *Atlas* plying between Bahia and Beira, the sanction port through which Rhodesia imported its oil. Peter felt sorry for the Royal Navy ships on the Beira patrol: the monotony must have been soul-destroying and there was little that the frigates could do other than ask questions. Backwards and forwards *Atlas* steamed, a gigantic carrier of oil, manned by an international crew. The master was Swedish: Captain Sven Christiansen, a huge man, with cropped red hair that bristled from his skull. He, too, was a 'loner', keeping himself in his cabin and aloof from day-to-day affairs. He spoke little and was harsh in his wielding of discipline. Peter's predecessor had crossed Christiansen's path and had summarily been paid off in Yokohama, thence to pay his own fare home.

The chief officer was French, Jules Lecroix, a taciturn Breton, who drank too much but who was ruthless and surprisingly efficient. The ship was deliberately undermanned to increase the company's profits, so the four watchkeepers shared the navigating, the senior, Alexis Popoulos, being the ship's navigating officer. The crew was bullied by Ernst Bueckner, a Pole from Eastern Germany, who cowered the motley collection of seamen who normally could endure no more than three voyages in this hell-ship. The one magnet that kept them was the lure of high pay.

Continuity was achieved by the presence of the master, the chief officer and, to a lesser extent, the four watch-keeping officers; Peter was now the junior, 'Philmore' being his immediate senior. In that situation, it was soon obvious to Peter that Morgan Finnimore craved for Peter's discharge from *Atlas* as soon as possible. Finnimore had patiently channelled his thoughts and energies to this one object and, after three months voyaging between Bahia and Beira, had succeeded in stirring up bad feeling against Peter.

The ship, it seemed, had always been divided against itself. The living conditions were not calculated to enhance contentment: the sparse conditions seemed deliberately imposed to ensure that no one would wish to stay long in *Atlas*. The cabins were of painted aluminium, the furnishings of grey metal alloy. There were no carpets, no curtains and only one steel chair on which to sit when off watch.

The messing was communal, on a cafeteria basis, and the food was monotonous, though there was enough to eat. In this heat, there was not enough fruit, insufficient vegetables in the diet and the choice was nil. With everyone stretched to the limit by the workload, there was no social contact except during the twenty-four-hour turn-rounds at the terminals. Men became irritable as the monotony wore on; not only were the routine, the heat and overwork rasping men's nerves, but the frustrations of language and the jealousies of multinationalities made life difficult.

In Milford Haven, where *Atlas* was discharging half her cargo before proceeding to Tranmere, Finnimore had returned the worse for wear from Neyland after the pubs had shut. He had several drunks with him and, reeling along the main deck, they had encountered Peter who, being duty officer, was sounding tanks.

'Get out've way, you ruddy druggie,' Finnimore had slurred. 'Still at it, are you, you little creep?'

Peter stood back, feeling the anger mounting inside him. The drunken idiot would stagger past and pass out in his cabin, so long as Peter refused provocation.

Finnimore turned towards the group of men behind him who, not understanding what was happening, were swaying on their feet and chuckling as they sensed a fight.

'Look at him, fellas,' Finnimore goaded. 'As smug as a bug in a rug.' Makin, the hulking Finn at the back of the circle, pressed forward, shoving his face into Peter's. 'Ger on m'boy. 'Tiz not standing fer that, 'er yer?' He shook his befuddled head. 'Ger on, boyo. Put up yer fists. Don't stand for et, from that bastard.' The others rollicked to and fro, savouring the tension.

'Shut up,' Peter said. 'You're all drunk. Get below; I'm not fighting anyone.' As he turned to walk away, a hand grabbed his shoulder and spun him around. It was Finnimore and there was murder in his eyes.

'I'll meet you tomorrow on the fo'c'sle head, Sinclair,' he slurred. 'When I'm not drunk. I'll knock the daylights out of you.'

There was an alcoholic cheer from the group around him. 'Garn, the creep hasn't got the guts,' the only Glaswegian in the ship growled. 'He's a coward.'

Peter's self-control crumbled. 'You hulking lout,' he snapped. 'I'll meet you on the fo'c'sle head when you've sobered up.' He faced Finnimore and stared him full in the face. 'I don't like bullies.'

Peter ducked as the bully swung at him. Finnimore overbalanced and fell to the deck, where he sprawled like a giant amoeba.

'Put him to bed,' Peter snapped, 'and get to hell out of here.'

To his relief, they shuffled off, leaving the unconscious Finnimore where he lay.

The tanker sailed on the morning tide, an hour before morning twilight. St Ann's Head lighthouse came abeam then passed down her starboard quarter, the beams of the red and white flashes hazy in the lowering visibility. She cleared the buoys of the middle channel rocks and, a mile to seaward, Peter lowered the ladder for the departing pilot. Though most of the V.L.C.C. tanker operators employed pilotage on passage from Milford to the Mersey, Globe economized by allowing their masters to make the passage, provided they laid their course outside The Smalls and kept to the separation zone of the shipping lanes. The shortcut between Grassholm and Skomer was unnecessarily constricted for a large tanker, though there was plenty of water.

As Peter climbed up the ladder to the boat deck, a seaman detached himself from the shadow beneath the lifeboat.

'Mr Philmore's waiting for you,' the man growled hoarsely, 'on the fo'c'sle head.'

Peter knew that this was a moment of decision. He would be acting insanely and realized full well that he was already, as an officer, breaking all the rules of discipline. Yet with rage boiling inside himself, he felt impelled to turn back, to retrace his steps down to the main deck and walk the long length to the fo'c'sle head. As an officer, he could be thrown out, his career ruined. He turned and rattled down the ladder, staring the seaman in the face. The man was laughing softly, a gleam of triumph in his eyes.

As Peter hurried forward along the green main deck, which was now slippery from the early morning haze, he shivered. The air was clammy, cold: fog was about.

CHAPTER 17: SEASONED WARRIORS

Captain Collingwood Kinane was weary. He was, he confessed to himself, at last ready to 'swallow the anchor'. He was tired and looking forward at least to abrogating the responsibilities of a ship's captain. As he leaned over the port wings of his old ship's bridge, he felt once again that both the ship and himself were, and always had been, inextricably bound together and complementary to one another.

Exmouth Haven was slipping down the Welsh coast, on passage from the Mersey to Cardiff, to unload her final cargo before being placed on the sale list, so for her too this was her last voyage. Collingwood Kinane was silent as the grey outline of Strumble Head came up through the dawn, fine on the port bow, with St David's Head and Ramsey Island beginning to show through the haze on the horizon. This could be the last time in his life that he'd sight these landmarks. Retired sea captains were like worn-out gloves: useless to anyone.

Tussok, his trustworthy and excellent navigating officer, was waiting beside him. He too would be leaving, because he had passed with flying colours his Extra Master's examination.

'Excuse me, sir,' Tussok interrupted tactfully, for, by now, the younger officer could sense his captain's moods before the Old Man knew them himself. 'You asked me to enquire whether you'd go inside The Smalls. We'll have to alter course in twenty minutes, sir, with this spring ebb under us.'

Kinane smiled briefly, a wintry grimace born of a lifetime of loneliness.

'D'ye not think I should have my last fling, eh, Mr Tussok?' he said jocularly. 'I've been making this passage for thirty-three years and should know it, shouldn't I? Radar okay?'

Tussok nodded. 'Working satisfactorily, sir. There's a bit of haze ahead,' and he jerked his head towards the southern horizon.

'Morning mist. Nothing about fog in the forecast,' Kinane added. 'I'll take her inside Grassholm. With this tide we'll be through in ten minutes.'

Tussok hurried back to his chart table, the look of disapproval betrayed by his open face.

'I'll show 'em,' Kinane muttered to himself. He looked up and shouted to the officer of the watch. 'Report when South Bishop is abeam to port, then alter course to pass inside Grassholm.' He raised his voice again. 'Course please, Mr Tussok?'

'One-six-o, sir,' the navigating officer called. 'That will take us slightly to the west of the centre line, but still keep us outside the twenty-fathom patch and its overfalls.'

Captain Kinane nodded. His officers and crew would have cause to remember their last voyage in *Exmouth Haven*: he'd demonstrate in no mean fashion that he was still in full possession of his faculties.

Half an hour later, with the light of South Bishop still flashing on *Exmouth Haven*'s port quarter, Captain Kinane was in the chart house checking his position. No turning back now: he was committed to the inshore passage. The owners ought to be grateful to their senior master; he'd be saving the company at least three hours on the passage. Luckily able seaman Ned Hindacre was on the wheel. That boy had done well: he was a good quartermaster and had qualified in the minimum of three years. He could easily become a ship master if that was his ambition.

Kinane looked up as he felt someone standing next to him. 'Well,' he snapped. 'What is it?'

'Right ahead,' Tussok reported. 'Fog bank, sir. Shall I reduce speed?'

Kinane nodded. 'Six knots,' he said. 'Set fog lookouts.' He glanced at the clock. It was precisely six thirty-three.

CHAPTER 18: DEEMED TO BE IMMINENT

On the *Atlas*'s bridge Captain Christiansen swore a Swedish oath. He had been caught out this time. Here he was, committed to this narrow channel off this desolate foreign coast of Wales, having made the passage only once before — and that, southbound. All would have been well if the radar had not failed at the critical moment, as Broad Sound came abeam to starboard and when he was well into the Grassholm Passage.

He had managed at first light to take a bearing of Skokholm, before the rocky island faded in the mist. The fix on Skokholm was unreliable because the radar went 'kaput' at the instant that a range was wanted. If Antonio Spirelli, that drunken Sparks, had not gone on the booze last night, he would never have allowed this radar circuit to blow. It was no good blaming anyone now. He, Christiansen, had to act — and quickly.

'Dead slow,' he commanded. 'Sound the siren.'

The officer of the watch (thank God it was one of the senior boys) flung open the bridge door and yanked at the lever. Fog swirled through the open doorway as the blast shattered the silence. Captain Christiansen waited impatiently for the five-second sound signal to terminate.

'Set fog lookouts,' he ordered. 'One up top and one in the eyes of the ship.'

He could have kicked himself for depending on a weather forecast. Visibility moderate, Wind Force 3 to 4, increasing to 6/7 later, they had said. With wind, who would expect fog? He wished that he'd never undertaken this passage: this was what came of trying to be clever, of trying to cut corners. He could not alter to starboard because of Skomer Island and he dare not get to hell out of it: there was scant room in this narrow passage in which to swing his enormous ship to port. The Smalls lay in wait, those jagged rocks that had claimed so many sailors' lives throughout the ages. There was a shout from the officer of the watch in the starboard wings where he was trying to sight Skomer.

'Overfalls, sir. Under the starboard bow.'

Christiansen felt the kick of fear in the base of his stomach. The soundings were twenty fathoms but, if he was inside the overfalls, he couldn't be far from the four-fathom patch which protruded at the western end of Skokholm.

'Port ten,' he commanded. 'Steer three-one-five.'

He'd have to come into the centre of the channel. The risk of collision was less than the hazard of grounding in fog on the rocks of Skomer.

Then from somewhere ahead, he thought he felt on his eardrums the reverberations of a ship's siren.

'Silence,' he snapped.

They opened the bridge doors and stood motionless, listening. The only sound was the thumping of the engines and the whistling of the breeze past the superstructure. Then, unmistakably, the boom of a ship's siren moaned on them from the fog right ahead.

The approaching ship must be on an opposite course, and she had a four-knot spring ebb under her. She must be proceeding at least eight or nine knots and, with *Atlas*'s four, the relative approach speed *must* be about twelve knots. She would have to maintain steerage way, even if she reduced speed drastically. *Atlas* should alter to starboard, but he dare not with Skomer so close.

'Sound "D" for Delta,' he snapped. He was manoeuvring with difficulty.

He peered ahead once again. He could see only up to the midship manifold: his bows were invisible in the fog. Beneath the water that bulbous bow must be protruding like a monstrous ram.

'Tell the fo'c'sle lookout to keep his phone in hand,' he ordered. 'Warn him to keep a sharp lookout.'

The officer of the watch picked up the telephone. The indicator light flickered. He waited a long ten seconds. He glanced at his captain.

'No reply, sir,' he said, his face white. 'No one on the phone in the eyes of the ship, sir.'

At that moment there was a long blast, right ahead. The low note boomed in the fog, very close now, fine on the starboard bow. Simultaneously, *Atlas*'s siren blasted out its warning 'D'.

'Stop engine,' Captain Christiansen snapped. The telegraph's tell-tale was repeated. The officer of the watch noted in the log that the time was six forty-two.

Someone had rigged up an impromptu boxing ring in the fo'c'sle head. A heaving line had been strung around the stanchions and in two opposite corners two steel chairs had been placed. As Peter pushed through the closed bulkhead door, he was surprised to see that the lights were on and that the onlookers were ready for him. Finnimore was already in his corner, stripped to the waist, his face grey from last night's debauch.

'Ten rounds,' someone said. 'And may the best man win.'

Peter discarded his jacket, stripped off his shirt. As he dipped below the rope, he heard the distant blast of the ship's siren. He was right then, fog *had* come down. That man who had passed him on his way for'd must have been the fog lookout hurrying to his post in the eyes of the ship. As Peter squared up to his opponent, a seaman struck the fire-alarm triangle. Finnimore moved forward, leering.

Peter put up his fists. He had boxed only in childish bouts in the gym where, instructed by the P.E. master, they had learned the basic arts of self-defence. Toe to toe, left arm outstretched; no one had told him how to combat the unorthodox southpaw like Finnimore who, had it not been for his self-indulgent living, could have become a good boxer. He was a loose-limbed fighter who came in close, both fists jabbing, crouched like a panther about to spring. He flung a quick right jab.

Peter felt the stinging pain across the bridge of his nose. His eyes watered involuntarily and there was derisory laughter from the onlookers circling the heaving line.

'C'm on, lad,' shouted the Irishman, Paddy Magnus. 'Thump the bastard, Philmore. What yer waiting for?'

Peter's mind raced. If he allowed Finnimore to fight inside his guard there was no chance. Peter's only hope lay in his fitness: he'd have to keep out of range and allow Finnimore to exhaust himself. Peter shot out his left and dabbed the taller man's nose. Finnimore checked, surprised, his eyes smouldering with anger.

'I'll murder you, Sinclair,' the bully panted as he came in, arms working like pistons. Peter danced backwards, guard up in the classical defensive position, left prodding away, trying to keep his opponent at his distance. It was no use; the heavier fighter bore through, brushing aside the continuous punches thrown by Peter.

A blow landed and the white paintwork swam before Peter's eyes. He weaved his head, ducking, staggering backwards, battling for time. There was hate in Finnimore's eyes as he charged forward, searching for the swift kill. Then the clang of the fire alarm and the onlookers dragged off the enraged Finnimore whose face, like his opponent's, was already bloodied.

Peter gasped, alone in his corner. He stood breathing deeply, trying to control his thoughts, to decide on his tactics. Then, a second before the second round began, the fo'c'sle head opened and a shaft of daylight poured inwards.

'Shut that door, will you?' Antonio, the Greek, yelled. The newcomer was Alfonso Biro, the young seaman from Buenos Aires, the man who had hurried for'd past Peter to his lookout post. He held the long telephone lead in his hand.

'What the devil are you doing down here?' Antonio persisted. 'You're on fog lookout.'

Alfonso swore and spat on the deck. 'Can't see my hand in front of me on the fo'c'sle,' he said. 'What's the point of being there? I want to see the fun.'

'Aw, come on, Antonio,' Magnus sang in his brogue. 'Let's be gettin' on with t' fight.'

The iron triangle rang again. Finnimore left his corner, cautious now, his arrogance waning. He'd have to box cannily; a quick, sharp lesson was what the boy needed and he, Finnimore, was going to administer it. He moved forward relentlessly, head down, the puny blows from the retreating youth bouncing off his skull. He jabbed, hooked, pulled, but the youngster was moving backwards, always a fraction beyond his reach.

'Stand up and fight, damn you,' Finnimore panted. He was tearing after Sinclair now, and then, as a left hook crunched home on the white face weaving in front of him, he laughed — a raucous, brittle sound that silenced the onlookers. *Not long now*, he thought; *I'll finish it immediately*. He took a deep breath, squared his massive shoulders and, arms hanging in front of him, he waded in. It was then that the telephone screamed.

Alfonso, the Argentinian lookout, scrambled out through the door. A long blast, followed by two shorts in rapid succession boomed through the fo'c'sle head deckhouse.

In the enclosed bridge of *Exmouth Haven*, Captain Kinane crouched over the luminous display of the radar's P.P.I. He had been staring at the rotating pencil of light until his eyes ached. There it was, the large blip on a steady bearing: dead ahead of him and closing remorselessly on collision course. The outline of The Smalls, the jagged profiles of Grassholm, Skokholm and Skomer were also plainly etched. An emergency of terrible magnitude was sweeping upon him.

'Stop both engines,' he growled. 'Full astern both.' He glanced at Hindacre, the quartermaster. 'Try to hold her,' he snapped. 'Report when you lose steerage way.'

Kinane could ease no farther over to the westward or he'd be on Grassholm. What the devil was this echo doing? The bearing remained steady, fine on his starboard bow — and it was a large echo, as big as a V.L.C.C.'s. Surely a crude carrier couldn't be coming through here in this fog?

A hooter boomed right ahead, very close now. One long blast followed by two shorts — 'D' for Delta: '*Keep clear of me. I am manoeuvring with difficulty.*' What the hell's she think she's doing?' Kinane muttered to himself. The engine room telegraph tinkled. The old ship began to shake as the worn-out diesels built up their revolutions.

'Three blasts,' the master snapped. 'Keep your eyes skinned.'

Tussok had jumped through the door and wrenched at the siren wire. The urgent signal echoed weirdly through the swirling fog.

Kinane stiffened, sensing the danger. Then, from out of the white mists, a dark mass emerged, swiftly, but very real. By the immensity of her slab side she must be a large tanker.

'My God!' the Captain shouted. 'I'm on her port bow. *She's turning to starboard!*'

Exmouth Haven's bow was invisible to the bridge. As her master ordered 'Hard-a-starboard', the ship shuddered. There was a moment of total silence. Captain Kinane stretched his arms forward to the bridge windows, as if to ward off the impending blow. Tussok bent his knees to absorb the shock. Hindacre turned away, his arms flailing at the wheel as he spun it hard-over. Then, like a sigh when the agony is over, the ship slowly began to heel, forced over on her side by a giant's hand.

Captain Kinane never heard the screaming metal: this was his last voyage wasn't it? His ship was dying, wasn't she? He shouted aloud, his oaths unintelligible. They were squeezing the life out of his ship and he was suffocating too.

CHAPTER 19: THE GALE

The silence on the bridge of *Atlas* was tangible. Captain Christiansen stood rooted to the deck, every sense strained to catch the first warning of the approaching ship. His mind raced as he imagined the several permutations that would suddenly be revealed to him. Full astern: she would swing out of control in this tide-race; hard-a-starboard: he was uncertain of his position and he was, he felt sure by the soundings of twenty-one fathoms, uncomfortably close to Skomer and Skokholm — he dare not alter far to starboard; hard-a-port: always the dangerous action to take. So long as the wheel was put to starboard, a board of inquiry would find it difficult to indict.

'Captain — there she is!'

The clipped accents of a South African lookout in the port wing ripped the silence. The fo'c'sle phone screamed. As Christiansen wrenched the instrument from its socket, he glimpsed a grey wedge bearing down on him, fine on the port bow and gliding straight towards him.

'Hard-a-starboard,' he commanded, his knuckles white as he gripped the bridge rail. 'Emergency full ahead. Sound one blast.'

He held his breath. He prayed: if there was a God, this was the moment to call upon His mercy. If *Atlas* could gather speed swiftly she might scrape past the bows now scything down upon her. The ship began to tremble as the propeller bit deep, slowly gaining revolutions.

The stem was swinging now — and, at last, *Atlas* was surging forward. The pointer of the log jerked — three — five — six knots. He'd have to check her swing as soon as he was clear and take off her speed, or he'd be on the rocks. He glanced to port.

The grey bows of a ship, splotched red along her plate lines, was less than fifty feet away; a rusty anchor was hanging on a level with *Atlas*'s number two lifeboat. Christiansen noted the buff line of her gunwales, the towering samson posts, the buff foremast and the old-fashioned tackles. A sailor was rigid by the rail; his mouth was open as he was pointing at the monster about to crush him. Christiansen turned away recoiling from the lethal ram. She would strike close forward of the bridge structure.

'To the starboard wings!' he yelled. 'Move! For God's sake, move!'

The impact came as he slithered to a stop by the starboard bridge door. The bows bit deeply into *Atlas*'s port side, on a ninety track, shearing with effortless ease through the grey steel. The stem rode upwards, to the cacophony of rending steel and crushing metal, as it carried everything before it. The advance gradually slowed until her bows became wedged over halfway across the V.L.C.C.'s deck. Then, with *Atlas* still making considerable way, the merchant ship slewed round, gouging her stem further into the body of the tanker. She lurched alongside *Atlas*'s port quarter, where she smashed all deck fittings and carried away all protrusions in both ships.

The shock broke free the cargo ship's starboard anchor. It careered from its hawsepipe and plunged into the bowels of the tanker. The rattling cable added its cacophony to the bedlam that raged between the two ships.

'My God!' Christiansen shouted, 'the engines!' He hurled himself at the engine room telegraph and yanked it twice to full astern. Ten of the longest seconds in his life elapsed as he waited for the explosion; in his imagination the flames were flickering for'd, bursting into the red glow that would herald the holocaust to follow.

He was peering through the for'd window when he was suddenly knocked from his feet. The ship shuddered, trembled the whole of her length. She was stopped.

'Stop engine!' he yelled at his officer of the watch. 'We're on the rocks!'

The depth recorder registered zero. She must have been almost stationary in that tide. The trembling eased. He dashed to the chart. They must be on the Head Bank, six cables west of Skokholm. Already he could feel the slow list to port.

'Send out a Mayday!' he shouted. 'Emergency Fire Stations.'

It was the prolonged blast on the siren that halted the fight in the fo'c'sle head. That, and the frantic shouting from Alfonso who was now battering on the deckhead above them.

As Peter stood back, he glanced around the faces of the spectators. Then, taking the lead from Antonio, they opened the door. Alfonso was peering outside when the whole ship began trembling. There was a sudden shock and the sound of screeching metal somewhere aft along the port side.

Peter ducked beneath the heaving line and grabbed his shirt. As he flung on his reefer jacket, there was another sickening juddering and, to add confusion, the crescendo of the Emergency Alarm.

'To your stations!' Finnimore shouted, fear in his voice. 'Quick about it.'

Peter was out before him, slithering and stumbling along the deck that was still shrouded in fog. He stopped with a jolt as he collided with a group of men ahead of him. They stood motionless, halted by the horror that lay ahead of them.

The bows of a merchant ship had sliced across nine-tenths of the tanker's beam. The bows were black and rusty and, as the seamen recoiled from the shocking sight, the anchor suddenly broke away to plunge downwards. As the cable plunged downwards, rust and dirt showering upwards in clouds of filth, a shackle snaked outwards.

Antonio, the Greek, had never been blessed with fast reactions. As he stood by the abyss, mesmerized by the swirling cavern beneath him, the cable flicked across his skull. With a scream he toppled backwards, his brains spilling on the deck where they all stood. He disappeared into the dark cavern, where the sea and the escaping oil bubbled and steamed in fury. This, strangely enough, was the instant in which Sinclair took charge. In this moment of horror, it was he who reacted instinctively.

'Back to the fo'c'sle!' he yelled. 'All of you — d'ye hear what I say?'

They stared for a moment at the young man, the cadet who had stood up to that bully Finnimore. At least the lad had guts. They turned and ran, stumbling, slipping and swearing until they had reached the ladder leading up to the fo'c'sle. They did not stop running until they had reached the eyes of the ship above the forepeak. Peter brought up the rear.

'Give me the phone,' he snapped. 'All of you, stand by the fire guns. Finnimore: start the emergency pumps.'

'Get stuffed, Sinclair,' the youth shouted. 'We don't want orders from you.'

Peter looked Finnimore straight in the eye. 'Finnimore, I'm in charge here. You've forfeited any respect. Now get cracking or I'll lock you in the searchlight room.'

For a long moment the two officers faced each other once more. That insane streak once again blazed in Finnimore's eyes as he fought to control himself.

'We only want one boss here,' Paddy Magnus, the Irishman, said. 'You'll do, Sinclair. You've got guts, man.' The burly seaman from County Clare spat on his hands. 'We'll follow you, *sir*.' But there was no sarcasm in the mark of respect.

In the awkward silence, Finnimore slunk away to lean over the starboard rail. He shouted, aware, too, that he could play a part:

'There's a dirty great rock over there, Sinclair. Look!'

There was no communication with the bridge and Peter replaced the phone. He hurried to the starboard bow. There, less than two cables distant, was the loom of an island. 'Too small for Skomer,' he said. 'Must be Skokholm.'

He turned then to collect his thoughts. He had counted seven men, excluding Finnimore and himself. The first two firefighters were already emerging from the fo'c'sle door when there were faint cries from the invisible bridge towering in the fog eight hundred feet away.

'*She's going*.' He heard the faint but familiar broken English of Captain Christiansen. 'Turn out the boats. Abandon ship.'

As the seamen turned to Peter, there was a shrieking of tormented steelwork being torn asunder. They stumbled aft then, impelled by terror to witness what they had all dreaded in their hearts. As Peter reached the midship manifold, he heard the fearful hissing of escaping gases, steam and water. Then, gurgling and crashing, the monster towering above them slipped slowly from sight. The starboard side of the ship opened, then stretched like elastic until it broke.

''Struth, sir — those overfalls—' Jan Dorp, the South African shouted. 'God Almighty.' The whole of the after part of the ship had broken free, wrenched off the bank by the overfalls of the spring ebb. There were the sounds of exploding boilers, surging seas, and men's screams growing fainter at every second.

Peter peered upwards again at the bows of the cargo ship looming above them. She was firmly embedded in what remained of *Atlas*, the forward three-quarters of her hull now balancing precariously on the Head Bank. He could hear faint shouts from the ship's fo'c'sle and then, peering more closely, he thought he could distinguish the white letters of her name on the bow: E-X-M-O— His pulse quickened. She couldn't be, surely? He could read no more, but he was suddenly certain that this was *Exmouth Haven*, his first ship.

Paddy, the Irishman, was crossing himself. The others were shocked into silence, staring at the space where their ship had been.

'Back to the fo'c'sle head,' Peter ordered. 'We'll wait for the fog to lift.'

He was surprised to find Finnimore still by the stem-head; he did not turn round when Peter and the others returned.

'Wind's getting up,' he said. 'That'll shift this ruddy fog.'

Peter felt apprehensive when the fog had cleared so swiftly; not by the heat of the sun, but because the wind force had increased so rapidly. Already the seas were boiling around the broken hulk and, he judged, there was plenty of wind out there: these confused seas were not only the result of the overfalls.

The rapid dispersal of the fog disclosed their true position. Four hundred yards on their starboard bow the black outline of Skokholm seemed horribly close. White seas broke around the base of the island; the overfalls hissed in their confusion; and a few miles to the northward the outline of Skomer showed plainly.

The cargo ship was visible now and she was certainly *Exmouth Haven*. Communications had been established between them because the Merchant Service still trained their men in the use of semaphore. By perching out on the port wings, an officer from *Exmouth Haven* had already passed messages. Could *E.H.* help? They could send across food by means of a Coston line-throwing gun. Were all survivors safe in *Atlas*? A Mayday had been transmitted: *Please report on the condition of the remains of Atlas.*

Peter judged that the starboard quarter of *Atlas* was bumping on the bank. She seemed to be pivoted at a point abaft the manifolds. The grounding had taken place on the second hour of the ebb. Perhaps, when the tide turned, she might break clear?

Mercifully, the bulkhead between numbers four and five tanks seemed to be holding. The sea was three-quarters up the side of the tank, which probably explained the miracle of her water-tightness: pressures inside and out were almost equalized.

The semaphore flags were flapping again from *Exmouth Haven*'s bridge:

'Gale eight to nine forecast,' he read. 'I am holed and am stuck fast in your port quarter. After gale, suggest we try to pump out oil to get off.'

Peter raised his right arm to the position of letter C: he had received and understood the message.

'Idiots,' Finnimore blurted. 'Don't they realize our pumping room is at the bottom of the sea?'

'They're only being helpful, sir,' Paddy said. 'What would you do, anyway?'

Finnimore remained silent. Peter said nothing, an idea germinating in his mind. The project was too impossible; no use even dwelling on it or mentioning it to the others.

Here they were, an intact hulk containing a million cubic feet of oil, balanced upon a bank on the edge of a beautiful stretch of the Welsh coast. A spark and the whole shebang could explode. A pierced hull and the hulk would remain stuck, its cargo slowly seeping out its two hundred thousand tons of oil. For either alternative, the whole of the western shores of the British Isles would be polluted for decades. The wild birds; the marine life; the fish — it was too ghastly to contemplate.

And *Exmouth Haven*? If there was fire, they'd be grilled alive. If she sank, at least they'd have a chance in the lifeboats. As for Peter and his band of survivors, what hope was there for them? A helicopter perhaps? It was too dangerous in this wind and with this list.

The tide, he realized from his passage planning with the navigating officer yesterday, was now reaching slack water. Another hour, and the ebb would be running. With the imminent southerly gale, wind would be against a spring ebb tide, so heaven help them in the mountainous seas that would build up.

Perhaps, if the wind moderated, helicopters could lift them off before they broke up? With no men on board, the greatest pollution disaster in the nation's history would inevitably follow. If seamen remained in the hulk, surely there was something they could do to prevent the appalling disaster? It was then, just as the semaphore flags began flapping again, that Peter realized there was a chance, however faint. Whether it could succeed depended on three factors: the gale; communications; and...

The semaphore flags were impatiently jerking into the 'Attention' position. The signalman in the port wings seemed agitated, so Peter must concentrate. He stood apart from the others and raised his right arm.

Frederick Carter had been first radio officer of *Exmouth Haven* for nearly three years. As he hurriedly took over his set from 'the second', the thought flashed across his mind that this was not the only occasion in this ship in which he had transmitted a Mayday distress call.

He flicked the switch to 2182 Kcs, watched the output needle build up, then pressed the transmit switch in the handle of his telephone instrument. He had to keep his voice cool and detached:

'MAYDAY, MAYDAY, MAYDAY,' he began. 'This is *Exmouth Haven*, *Exmouth Haven*, *Exmouth Haven* ... Mike Oscar Kilo Victor, Mike Oscar Kilo Victor, Mike Oscar Kilo Victor.'

Carter removed the pressure from the handset. He glanced at the loudspeaker, willing a response. There was a crackle, and then the calm and confident voice of the Shore Station, Milford Haven Radio:

'*Exmouth Haven*, this is Milford Haven Radio. Your MAYDAY received. Over.'

Communication with the outside world was established. Carter nodded at his second radio officer. 'Tell the master,' he murmured.

Seconds later Captain Kinane was standing by Carter's side. He nodded and the radio officer rose from his chair.

'This is the master speaking,' Captain Kinane began.

At that moment the ship shuddered and her forepart jerked in the bowels of the V.L.C.C. Captain Kinane rose swiftly, handed back the telephone to Carter and hastened to his bridge. He had dreaded the turning of the tide. As he reached the bridge windows his heart sank: his worst fears were being realized.

The ebb was now running fast. The force of the stream was working upon her in an opposite direction and forcing her after part farther towards the shoal water. She was still afloat aft, but what would happen when the full strength of the ebb began to run? Only a miracle could save them from being set fairly and squarely on the bank. With the gale reported to be imminent, *Exmouth Haven* would be pounded to pieces.

Captain Pelly was shaking hands with the outward Liverpool pilot who, having cleared the Bar light vessel, was anxious to re-embark in the pilot boat bobbing alongside the port side. The radio was crackling in the wheelhouse when the desultory conversation was broken by a tense, dramatic message: MAYDAY, MAYDAY, MAYDAY...

The master listened attentively. He shook his head, then nodded at his officer of the watch.

'Half ahead,' he ordered. 'Set course to clear Point Lynas.'

A distress call always dismayed Captain Pelly, of S.S. *Marlin*, of the Pisces tanker fleet. He knew only too well the urgency behind the laconic signal; the agonies perhaps being endured at this moment by the unhappy master and his crew. He walked to the chart house at the after end of the wheelhouse where he peered over the chart.

Marlin had discharged at Tranmere and was now on her way to Lyme Bay to lighten another V.L.C.C., *Stingray*, inward bound from the Gulf. At full speed *Marlin* could be off The Smalls rock within six hours.

Captain Pelly's pulse quickened. He always secretly enjoyed the challenge of an emergency. Here he was, ideally placed to render assistance if it was required. Though a tanker in ballast was normally an unwieldy vessel, *Marlin* handled excellently and Captain Pelly knew, inside himself, that he was a tolerably competent seaman. Thoughtfully he wandered into the radio office where, requesting permission from his radio officer, he picked up the telephone transmitter.

Peter was surprised at the ease with which he was able to command his small band of men. Even Finnimore seemed to be resigned, though, Peter noted, Paddy Magnus stood never far behind him. Perhaps the horror of Antonio's death had brought them all to their senses?

When the tide turned southerly, Peter detailed the seven men into two watches, the first in the charge of Finnimore, the second under himself. Two men were to stay on watch, the other two off-watch sheltering beneath the fo'c'sle head. Those off-watch were to sleep and use as little energy as possible, for with the first pangs of hunger, morale was already beginning to deteriorate. The eight-to-twelve had gone on watch when Peter saw the foremast and derricks of *Exmouth Haven* suddenly begin to shake. The scrunching of metal grew in intensity where the ships were interlocked. Were they both breaking up?

The cause of the maelstrom was the spring ebb which had begun to run and which was now running fast against the wind. The seas were building up in wild confusion, with some of the crests leaping upwards to break over the starboard gunwales. The force of the stream would soon push *Exmouth Haven* farther on to the bank. Peter looked up and there was her signalman again, flapping his semaphore flags.

Exmouth Haven had immediately recognized the danger. Men were already gathering on their fo'c'sle where they were working with haste. With hooks and tackles they fleeted the starboard cable, having catted its anchor. Not until a wire had been passed across to *Atlas*, did *Exmouth Haven* begin to weigh her port anchor which had disappeared into the depths of *Atlas*'s mangled compartment.

Through the brief semaphore messages, Peter understood that *Exmouth Haven* was coming on *Atlas*'s port side. By taking the cargo ship's starboard cable-end outboard of the tanker; and by securing it on the bitts by the break of *Atlas*'s fo'c'sle head, *Exmouth Haven* would be able to haul herself slowly ahead until she was abreast *Atlas*'s manifolds.

Peter turned to both his watches and, by means of the emergency diesel generator in the fo'c'sle head, was able to power the for'd winch. By using a 2½-inch wire, they slowly hauled the cable through the port fairleads where it was secured to the bitts. The huge fenders were then turned out and lowered over the side from their davits.

Exmouth Haven then broke her port cable and, by going full astern and heaving in on her starboard cable was able to tear herself free of the stranded remains of the tanker. Then, foot by foot, she edged up alongside until she lay, bucking and surging on her doubled-up back springs, some thirty feet clear of *Atlas*. The tidal stream rushed between the two ships but, by steaming slowly ahead on her port propeller, *Exmouth Haven* was able to maintain her position. Captain Kinane was leaning over the starboard wing and bellowing instructions through his megaphone.

Though the wind was now Force 6, the gale was not expected until the evening. It was now raging in area Shannon and its centre appeared to be advancing at about fifteen knots. Pisces's lightening tanker, *Marlin*, was coming to their aid and should be here soon after low water. She was in ballast and there was ample water for her to use *Exmouth Haven* as a gigantic catamaran. *Marlin* would attempt coming along *Exmouth Haven*'s port side where she would secure safely enough by using her special lightening fenders. If conditions allowed, she would pass her two large transfer hoses across *Exmouth Haven.*

'What type of hose connections d'you use?' Kinane shouted across. It was at this moment that he recognized his one-time deck cadet. He waved in acknowledgement, but was too intent on speed for the niceties.

'American type, sir,' Peter yelled back. 'Please tell *Marlin* that we know how to secure them.'

'Right,' the captain of *Exmouth Haven* replied. 'We've got to move fast to beat the gale.' He laid down the megaphone, then picked it up again as an afterthought struck him.

'Can you use your crane?' he yelled.

'No, sir. No power.'

'I'll use my derricks,' Kinane replied. 'If the gale hits us whilst transferring, we'll have to break away — let go everything and stand clear.'

'Aye, aye, sir.' Peter waved back, smiling bitterly. Kinane continued:

'If we can transfer enough to lighten you sufficiently, I'll try to ease you off using my own engines. Salvage tugs are on the way.' The master then disappeared from the bridge. In the silence that followed, nothing but the surge of the tidal stream between the two ships could be heard.

Peter walked away slowly from the spray-drenched rail. His mind felt numb from tiredness and tension; every scrap of willpower was needed now to prepare the gear in *Atlas* for the quick connection of the transfer hoses: his men were exhausted. Crisply he gave his orders. The men responded, silently turning to set up the tackles and prepare the connectors. Finnimore stood ostentatiously on the fo'c'sle, hands in pockets and peering down at the toiling men. Peter stood apart from the others, encouraging and checking whilst he sifted his thoughts. He felt Finnimore's eyes upon him but by now Peter had ceased to care. The fellow was insane.

If *Marlin* could beat the gale, there was a distant chance that *Atlas* could be lightened sufficiently for her to be nudged off the shoal. At high water she had seemed to be rocking on the edge of the bank; lightened by some ten feet, she should surely float clear if she had not made more water. Even if she was badly holed, little additional water could flood into the hulk because her tanks were already full of oil. Once clear of the bank, she might float long enough for them to jump for their lives, even if *Exmouth Haven* and *Marlin* had broken away. The lifeboat would surely be arriving soon, but there were no life jackets up here: all the life-saving equipment had been stowed in the living quarters aft.

For the first time on this day, Peter felt the finger of death upon them. He pushed the thought away. Provided *Marlin* arrived soon, and if he could connect the hoses at least two hours before the gale, enough oil could be pumped out to lighten her the few feet necessary to float off. There was a chance, but it was desperately slender. Truth, they said, was stranger than fiction, but what an extraordinary coincidence it was that both *Exmouth Haven* and *Marlin* should be involved.

Both ships that he had served in — and the knowledge that he had acquired in *Marlin* could yet save all their lives.

Again he felt Finnimore's eyes upon him. The fellow surely was mad? He certainly could not be trusted to pull his weight. As Peter turned to clamber up the ladder to try and placate Finnimore, he heard the low booming note from the siren of a large modern ship. He glanced across the water to the north-west. There she was, that spotless and proud ship, *Marlin*, a plume of white wisping from her funnels. She was turning towards them and along her port side hung festoons of lightening fenders. To the westward, the grey clouds were scudding in from the Atlantic; the sea was green and the waves were breaking white.

CHAPTER 20: THE MADMAN

The waiting was the worst of the tension: the nine men in the stricken tanker were now huddled by the break in the fo'c'sle, where they sheltered from the rain that drove in curtains of water across the surface of the sea. These men had been without food for fifteen hours; they had toiled unceasingly and were cold and afraid as they watched the towering freeboard of the lightening tanker bearing down upon the port side of *Exmouth Haven.*

'If she lays on too hard,' Paddy muttered, 'we'll be done for. She'll push us hard on the bank.'

'Why don't we jump for it?' Bruno, the Latvian pleaded. 'Better than being crushed here, or waiting to be burnt alive.'

Finnimore's voice cut in:

'Because our little hero wants to save the ship, man.' His eyes were wild as he looked around them all. 'We ought to jump. They'll lower a boat to pick us up.'

The Latvian nodded his head, but Paddy Magnus growled:

'I'll break anyone's neck if he quits now,' he said. 'Ye'll all obey Mr Sinclair or we're all done for.' He walked towards Finnimore: 'D'ye understand, sorr?'

'Be careful, Magnus,' Finnimore shouted, his mouth twitching, 'or I'll run you in.'

Peter sensed that this was the one moment when all could be lost — by their own lack of discipline.

'Stand by the lines,' he shouted. 'Shut up and look slippy. Watch out — here she comes!'

They could hear faintly the cries of the men who were sending out the ropes and wires to *Exmouth Haven*. The seas between the three ships were now raging, an ugly confusion of white foam. There was barely a perceptible shudder as *Marlin* nudged the cargo ship, portside-to and stemming the flood.

'She's done it!' Magnus shouted. 'Begorra, she's done it,' and a cheer from the small band of men on board *Atlas* drifted away on the wind.

Marlin was swiftly secured. Her vast ship's side lurched up and down, pitching in the seaway. *Exmouth Haven*, too, was yawing and jerking on her springs. Captain Kinane was trying to catch Peter's attention.

'Stand by the hoses,' he yelled. 'They're coming over.'

Rearing above the chasm between the two ships was *Exmouth Haven*'s starboard for'd derrick. From its head was slung a stirrup from which the huge transfer hose hung down like an elephant's trunk. In the swell, it danced about like a winnowing flail.

'Stand clear!' Peter yelled. 'Set up the steadying lines.'

As the hose swung across, Peter was careful to stand from under but, once the end was within six feet of the manifold, he rushed forward towards the Irishman.

'Lower the bight,' he yelled, looking upwards to *Exmouth Haven*. 'Adjust the height on the scope.'

Magnus watched over him like a wet nurse. When a particularly bad swell rolled the ships together, the huge Irishman picked Peter up bodily and yanked him from the lethal trunking.

Peter struggled with the flange, his muscles like iron bands as they cramped. Each time he lined up the first bolt with the hole in the flange, another sheer would lift the nose clear. A second's misjudgement and he would lose his hand, let alone his fingers — then, with a quick flick, the first nut was on. A swift turn with the quick-acting lever and the patent connector was made. He slithered clear on all fours, away from the murderous hose.

The Irishman grinned as those on the steadying lines walked back with them. The stirrup took the weight and, after adjusting the plumb by using the derrick guys, Peter ordered the valves to be opened.

'Ready to pump on the first hose,' he yelled exultantly. An answering hand waved back (surely that was Pounder?) and seconds later the hose began to pulsate. Finnimore, who had descended from the fo'c'sle head to attend the vents, looked up briefly and nodded.

'Full speed,' Peter yelled. 'Give her the gun.'

He watched anxiously as the hose jumped and heaved. With the present movement between the ships, it was barely safe to continue.

'Ready for number two?' Pounder, for now Peter could recognize him, bawled across the angry gap. 'Haul away.'

Once again the operation was repeated. It was easier now, having learned the snags from the first connection. The adaptor flicked home without a hitch. They jumped clear and Peter stood back, a note of triumph in his voice as he yelled:

'Pump on number two.'

There was another cheer as the second hose began to suck. The incredible had happened. By a superb feat of seamanship, Captain Pelly and Captain Kinane had successfully completed the first phase of the operation. Peter looked up as Pounder shouted through his megaphone across the water.

'Double up the back spring.' His words floated down on the wind. 'Watch out for the turn of the tide.'

The spring was a six-inch nylon hurricane hawser: the emergency diesel generator had coughed its last, so the hawser had to be hauled over by hand. Finally, the fore spring was made fast on the bitts of the fo'c'sle head.

Peter took the men back to the shelter of the break. Not until she had lightened about six feet of draught could there be any chance of getting off. There was nothing to do but wait.

Some tried to sleep, crouched in any corner out of the wind. In their sodden clothes, at best they reached half-consciousness. Others crouched on their haunches, staring at the hoses; some shut their eyes and prayed.

Peter must have been dozing. He no longer cared about his own life. If the Good Lord was to snatch him now, so be it. As his mind wandered, he gradually became aware of two different sensations: there was a spasmodic trembling, a shuddering at intervals, running the whole length of the hulk; and, like a blast from the rear of a jet engine, a violent wind squall which shrieked through the rigging of the three ships.

Suddenly *Atlas* had become alive, Peter rushed aft to the manifold, to shout across to *Exmouth Haven*, his words blown away on the wind.

'She's afloat!' he roared. 'She's moving,' and he pointed to the mangled mass of steel on the starboard quarter. Pounder waved back as if he understood. Seconds later, the small figure of Captain Kinane appeared in the starboard wing of his bridge.

'I'm going to try and move you,' the master called. 'Stand clear.'

The derricks were now thrashing crazily, tons of steel tube snatching against the guys, as the ships pitched and rolled in the sudden worsening of conditions.

'She's free, sorr,' Magnus yelled. 'Sure, she's free.'

The steel groaned, yielded to the pressures, screeched as it sundered. The cargo ship alongside went ahead, then steamed astern. *Atlas* whipped from the stresses but still she was stuck.

'She must be impaled,' Peter said, talking to himself. 'Surely she'll come off now?' As he looked aft, he froze to the deck where he stood. A hump of metal was suddenly bulging upwards. The ridge ran transversely across the deck, terminating at the base of the port crane.

'My God!' Paddy shouted above the wind. 'She's broken her back.'

Peter barely heard the warning. The wind was now of gale force strength, a raging fury intent on destroying these puny, man-made ships. Another ten minutes' pumping and they might yet be free. Oh God, how near to deliverance — why desert us now?

He had to turn away, his face, he knew, reflecting the anguish now swamping him. Another few minutes ... he knew that Captain Pelly would continue pumping until the last moment. But the breakaway would be hazardous in the extreme. A careless casting-off, with the ships scraping each other, and *Marlin* would erupt in a ball of fire. A few more minutes.

'*Stop him, sir.*'

Paddy Magnus was shouting, his face was white and he was staring for'd. 'The officer's gone berserk, sir.' He had already started to scramble for'd but Peter overtook him, leaping up the fo'c'sle ladder towards the insane man.

Finnimore stood astride the port bitts. His massive chest was flung back and in his arms was an axe, evidently snatched from the for'd emergency fire station. His cap had gone and his flaxen hair streamed in the wind. His eyes were wild and he was screaming gibberish. He was facing the advancing men and, as they stopped in their tracks, he swung again at the nylon hawser. The blade snicked the rope and a nylon strand peeled backwards, like a broken violin string.

'Stand back!' he roared. 'I'm the master, d'ye hear. Captain Finnimore—' and the wild laughter floated away on the wind.

'Come on, Paddy,' Peter shouted. 'Get him.'

He knew then that his life was in the balance as he hurled himself in a rugger tackle for Finnimore's legs. He saw the glint of steel, felt it crash into the deck. He heard a cry as Paddy tripped and fell, his weight bowling against Finnimore's thighs.

Peter clung to the madman's legs, so close that the blade of the axe could not reach him. Suddenly he felt Finnimore's body begin to lose balance. The axe swung again and Peter kicked with all his strength to evade the flashing blade. A swish! and the axe bit into the nylon hawser.

There was a fluttering like a shell tumbling through the air; a crack! like a gun exploding; and then a scream that hung on the wind. Peter glimpsed the white flash of the nylon rope springing back on itself, recoiling and flailing everything in its path. Finnimore, standing directly in line, was flung against the rails, the wind knocked out of him as he hung like a sack, head-down over the side.

CHAPTER 21: THE DERELICT

They lifted Peter down the ladder, held him until his trembling limbs slowly took his weight. It was the South African, Jan Dorp, who spoke first.

'You're all right, sir.' He paused, then continued: 'C'mon, sir. We need you.'

Peter heard the clipped words. He shook his head, nausea sweeping over him. Above the wind a man shouting: a distant voice, from another world.

'BREAKAWAY' … Pounder: that's right, the mate's voice.

There was a shattering report as the fore-spring parted; then the head rope, whistling through the air.

'Disconnect,' Pounder was yelling. 'We're slipping our cable.'

The urgency brought Peter to his senses. He knew that they were finished. If they had to die, they might as well try to save the other ships. Dear God, he must shut off the valves, disconnect the adaptors.

'Shut the valves,' he yelled at Jan Dorp. 'Come on, you layabouts, help me with the connectors.'

He hurled himself at the huge flanges. *To hell with the danger*, he thought: *disconnect, let go, or we'll roast alive.*

He grabbed the first lever and pulled. A bolt wrenched clear; there was a crack and the hose leaped upwards. Another wrench, and the second had gone. Recklessly he stood up and watched the lines parting like pack-thread, the air a whirl of flailing booms and wires. Already the gap between *Exmouth Haven* and the hulk was beginning to widen. He could glimpse the seas now, a raging torrent of confused water, further beneath them than a few hours earlier.

Atlas had shuddered. Perhaps it was the blow of *Exmouth Haven*'s quarter against their side that did it? Her motion was suddenly different, more regular. As he watched, the ridge across the deck began moving. The ship was whipping, moving to the swell.

'We're off!' Peter yelled. 'We're ruddy well afloat.'

There was no response from the exhausted men. The ridge was cracking, splitting wide and slowly opening across the deck. They watched, horrified. The hulk was definitely afloat again, swept off the bank by the returning tidal stream of the flood. She was moving through the water, the black islet of Skokholm sliding past the blue hills of Wales beyond.

'Look at that, sir.' Jan Dorp was nodding towards the starboard bow. Skomer stood up menacingly, black, with a white circlet foaming at its base. The hulk, its after portion hinged at the keel and its back broken, was being swept out of control through the narrow channel and on to the jagged rocks.

'We'd all better pray,' Jan Dorp said quietly, 'as we've never prayed before.' He made the sign of the cross and bowed his head in silence. The others followed his example: there were no atheists now, with twenty minutes left to live. Peter lifted his eyes skywards.

The low clouds were scudding across the grey sky, a sombre multitude in endless procession from the west. Peter shivered from the wet, the cold and the wind. He felt detached, an outsider looking in. Would it be cold, as he drowned, and what would the sensation be like? Or would she erupt in a sheet of fire? They'd be warmer then…

He thought they were gulls at first, a couple of gannets perhaps, searching for fish, scudding the wave-tops with that superb flight of theirs, wing tips kissing the breakers as the birds swooped down the troughs. The two specks seemed too steady for gannets, perhaps they were —

'*Choppers*,' someone yelled. 'C'mon, fellas — down to the pad.'

'It's the RAF,' Peter said. 'Divide into watches. Dorp,' and he called to the South African, 'you take the first watch.'

The specks in the sky were growing larger at every second. Then the first helicopter was over them, hovering like a gigantic vulture, its rotors generating a violent turbulence upon them. Down snaked a recovery wire, a belt and a snatch-hook dangling on the end.

They sent Finnimore up first; the man was mad, but now he was a pathetic creature, suddenly docile and with listless eyes. Dorp hooked him on and they watched him spiralling upwards, a limp figure, uninterested in his fate. They saw him bundled over the lip of the cabin, where he was grabbed by the waiting crew. The pilot was plainly visible, face turned towards them, immobile in concentration,

'Good old RAF,' Peter breathed. He saw the first watch go. Then with the roar of the breakers growing louder at every minute, in came the second chopper. Peter hooked on Paddy first; then up went the next three, while he waited for his own lift. Down came the wire; so fragile it seemed. He felt the jerk as his feet left the deck. The helicopter swung away, climbing as he spiralled upwards, like a marionette on a string. Beneath him, he could see *Marlin* out to the westward and, close to her, old *Exmouth Haven* who seemed down by the bows.

The long hulk of the remains of *Atlas* was now within two cables of Skomer. Her stem was caught in the maelstrom, the seas angrily cascading over her bows. She disappeared in a seething mass of white, raging seas and he turned away — none of them would have lived through that.

A hand grabbed his collar and, with a lurch, he was scrambling over the edge of the helicopter's recovery door.

'You're all right now, mate,' a gruff Yorkshire voice said. 'Look — so's your boat…' The sergeant was pointing downwards, a grin on his leathery face.

Five hundred feet below, what appeared as a great barge, was swinging round in the tidal stream. The stern of *Atlas*'s hulk was pivoting outwards, her bows steady, held in a back-eddy. As Peter watched, the whole length of her spun free, like a twig in a mountain stream, tossed clear of Skomer as the massive hull swept northwards. There, a mile or so away, their navigation lights already twinkling in the dusk, were two ships, pitching and yawing in the swell.

Atlas's hulk was safe. These were two salvage tugs, waiting like sheepdogs to gather her up and take her in tow.

CHAPTER 22: IN SURE HANDS

When Peter reached home, there were two letters waiting for him on the chest of drawers in his room. In a corner of the envelope of the first was the neat logo of the Globe Tanker Company. He slit open the letter and out fell a cheque. He picked it up and ran downstairs with it. His father stood in the sitting room, his back to the fireplace, smoking his pipe.

'It's yours, Dad,' Peter said.

His father glanced at it; his bushy eyebrows formed two half-moons of surprise.

'Humph,' he murmured. 'The interest wasn't as much as all that.' He handed the cheque back to his son.

Peter twice read the figures: two hundred and twenty pounds. Then he glanced at the small statement sheet. 'To one month's salary,' he read. 'One hundred and twenty pounds. In appreciation of services rendered to the Company: one hundred pounds.'

'Good grief,' he said. 'That's good of 'em.' He thrust the correspondence back into his father's protesting hand. 'I'm more stubborn than you are, Father. Take the lot, call it interest for services rendered.'

'Humph,' the older man said. Then, 'Humph,' again. He was gazing out into the garden where the first signs of September were touching gold the poplar leaves. He watched his son who had now opened the second letter. The youth had matured into a man in such a short time. Gone was the adolescent uncertainty, the youthful, unlined face. Instead, here was a seasoned man, quietly confident, who know where he was going.

There were already lines at the corners of his eyes, and there was a thoughtfulness about him. The dark hair was shorter and there was a new-found smartness about him.

'It's from Captain Pelly,' his son said quietly. 'He wants me back as fourth officer.' The brown eyes were alight with happiness.

'Will you go? I thought you'd given up the sea after this last experience.' The older man was probing, a glint in the wise old eyes.

'Of course I'll go.' Peter had moved over to the window, his hands on his hips and leaning forward, in that stance that his father knew so well.

'It's been a long three years, Dad, since I first joined. Remember?' and he turned briefly to smile at his father. 'That old girl, *Exmouth Haven*: she was falling apart, dirty and old-fashioned. But, with all her faults, I loved her. She taught me more than any other, so far. She taught me seamanship, and power of command. She showed me how good the modern cargo ships can be — those ships of the major companies, Port Line, the Clan Boats, Blue Funnel — they're great ships! Captain Kinane and his officers — they were a grand bunch, looking back on it all.'

'Will you settle for tankers?' The father was questioning, making sure.

Peter nodded. 'It won't be Globe though, Dad. It's difficult to forget that last voyage.'

The older man laid his hand on his son's shoulder. There was a long silence between them as they watched the shadows lengthening across the lawn.

'It's a different life at sea, Dad. There's no sham. It's real, close to the fundamentals. Life may be hard at times, but the sea calls me — I can't give it up, can't chuck it, just like that.' He turned to his father, his eyes questioning, serious. 'D'you understand?'

The grey-haired man nodded, looked away.

'You can't escape,' he said. 'It's in the blood.'

GLOSSARY OF NAUTICAL TERMS

ABAFT — nearer the stern than the object referred to, e.g. abaft the capstan.
ABEAM — at right angles to the fore and aft line, amidships.
AFT — towards the stern.
ALOFT — up the mast or in the rigging.
ASTERN — in the rear.
ATHWART — across or from side to side.
ATHWARTSHIPS — across the ship; at right angles to the fore and aft line.
AWEIGH — the moment when the anchor is broken from the ground.
BALLAST — extra weight stowed in a ship for added stability.
BEAM — the breadth of the ship.
BILGE — the part of the ship inboard near the keel.
BOLLARD — an upper deck fitting with two heads to which wires and hawsers are secured.
BOOT-TOPPING — the line between wind and water which is usually painted with anti-fouling of a different colour.
BOW — the parts of the ship's sides most near to the stem.
BOWER ANCHOR — the main anchor.
BRAIL — a wire or rope which encircles a sail or net for gathering-up purposes.
BROW — a portable bridge, which is sometimes covered, connecting the ship to the shore.
BULKHEAD — a vertical partition between decks which separates one compartment from another.

BULWARKS — the plating around the edge of the upper deck which prevents men or gear being washed overboard.

CAPSTAN — a machine, driven either electrically or by steam, with which to weigh anchor or to haul in a hawser.

CHAINS — the platform extending on either side of the ship, generally on the upper deck abreast the bridge on which the leadsmen stand to heave the lead when taking a sounding.

CON — to direct the steering of the ship.

CUTTER — a fore-and-aft rigged boat with one mast, a mainsail and foresails.

DECK HEAD — the overhead surface beneath the deck.

DERRICK — a spar which is fitted with tackles for lifting purposes.

DISPLACEMENT — the weight of a ship.

DRAUGHT — the depth of the lowest point of the keel below the ship's waterline.

EYES OF THE SHIP — the extreme fore-ends of the ship near the navel pipes.

FAIRLEAD — an upper deck fitting through which a rope is rove in order to alter the lead.

FALLS — the boat's falls are the tackles used for hoisting a boat at the davits.

FLARE — the curve outwards of the ship's side forward.

FLUSH DECK — when the deck is a continuous unbroken line from stem to stern.

FORE AND AFT LINE — the line from stem to stern in line with the keel.

FORECASTLE OR FO'C'SLE — that part of the upper deck which lies forward.

FO'C'SLE HEAD — the fore-part of a merchant ship; the anchors, cables and winches are worked from the fo'c'sle head.

FOREFOOT — that part of the stem lying between the water-line and the fore end of the keel.

FOREMAST — the forward mast.

FOUL ANCHOR — when the anchor is snarled by the cable or has picked up a wire.

FREEBOARD — the height of a ship's side above the waterline.

GANG PLANK — a plank stretching between two ships, or from a ship to the jetty upon which to walk.

GRIPES — matting with thimbles and lanyards with which to secure a boat at the davits.

HAWSE PIPE — the pipe leading to the cable locker through which the anchor cable runs.

HEEL OF THE SHIP — the angle of a ship from the perpendicular.

HOUSED — the mast is housed when partly lowered down.

JURY MAST — a temporary mast fitted in an emergency.

KEDGE ANCHOR — an auxiliary and lighter anchor.

KNOT — measurement of speed. 1 knot = 1 nautical mile (6080 ft.) per hour.

LANYARD — a short rope, generally used for setting up rigging.

LAZY GUY — an additional guy which is fitted to a boom for securing purposes when the ship rolls.

LIST — if a ship heels permanently she is said to have a 'list on'.

MAINMAST — the mast abaft the foremast.

MAST HEAD — the top of the mast.

MIDSHIPS — the centre part of the ship.

MIZZEN MAST — the aftermost mast.

NAVEL PIPE — the hole fitting on the forecastle through which the anchor cable runs to the hawse pipe and down to the cable locker.

PELORUS — a gyro compass fitted with a bearing ring and mounted on the bridge.

PENDANT — a long shaped flag which is narrower at the outer end: usually numerals, manoeuvring or special pendants to indicate the various stages in weighing and anchoring.

POOP DECK — the part of the upper deck which is at the stern.

PORT — the left-hand side of the ship looking forward.

QUARTER — the after part of the ship's side near the stern.

RAKE — the angle of a funnel or mast from the perpendicular in the fore and aft line.

RATLINES — ropes seized horizontally on to the shrouds in order to form a ladder.

R/T — radio telephone.

SCOTCHMAN — a length of steel or wood used to prevent chafing.

SCUPPER — holes in the bulwarks which allow the water to drain from the upper deck.

SCUTTLES — circular 'windows' or portholes in the ship's side.

SHEER — the curve of the deck at the head and stern above the midship portion.

SHROUDS — the wire ropes supporting a mast in the athwartships direction.

STANCHION — a vertical metal support for guard rails, awnings, etc.

STANDING RIGGING — fixed rigging such as the shrouds and stays.

STARBOARD — the right-hand side of the ship looking forward.
STAY — the wire ropes supporting a mast in the fore-and-aft direction.
STEM — the foremost part of the ship.
STERN — the aftermost part of the ship.
TAFFRAIL — the rail around the stern.
TOPGALLANT MAST — a small mast fitted above the topmast.
TOPMAST — the upper part of a mast, generally a separate spar.
TRIATIC STAY — a wire rope between the foremast and mainmast mastheads.
TRIM — the angle in the fore-and-aft line at which a ship floats.
TRUCK — a small circular horizontal fitting on the extreme top of the mast.
TUMBLE HOME — if the sides of a ship incline inwards near the upper deck they are said to 'tumble home'.
UNDER WAY — when a ship is neither made fast nor aground, she is said to be under way.
UP AND DOWN — the anchor cable is 'up and down' when it is vertically taut from the anchor to the bow.
VANG — a rope or wire controlling the outboard end of a gaff.
W/T — Wireless/Telegraphy.
WAIST — the part of the upper deck amidships which lies between the fo'c'sle and the quarter deck.
WINDLASS — a type of capstan, with horizontal drums, for hoisting and hauling.
YARD — horizontal spars set athwartships on the mast to carry signal halyards and W/T aerials, etc.

A NOTE TO THE READER

Dear Reader,

If you have enjoyed the novel enough to leave a review on **Amazon** and **Goodreads**, then we would be truly grateful.

SAPERE
BOOKS